LEVITATE

Geonn Cannon

Supposed Crimes LLC • Matthews, North Carolina

www.supposedcrimes.com

This book is typeset in Goudy Old Style.

Special Thanks to Imelda May, whose song Levitate inspired the title of this novel.

PROLOGUE

Berlin 1983

MARTA GRESHAM was three years and two months old when she died.

She was standing on a street corner not far from the Wall, a little tipsy, holding the hand of her boss, the man with whom she'd been having an affair. They were playfully debating whether she would go left, toward her apartment, or right, toward his. It was more likely they would end up at his apartment since it was her intention to spend the night with him, but she didn't want to make it look too easy.

"It's very late." She hid her coquettish smile behind the upturned collar of her coat.

Stan Voigt returned the smile and pretended to cinch the coat tighter at her throat as an excuse to touch her. "All the more reason for you not to walk the streets alone. So many horrible things can happen to a young woman on her own."

That comment made her look past him, made her take note of the man walking fast on the other side of the street. She noticed him the way she noticed everything else, but she didn't mark him as a threat. She was too focused on what she would say next. How to surrender to his sloppy flirtation without giving away her eagerness. So she looked into his eyes with love and desire, ignoring his unkempt eyebrows and the thick bulb of his nose, or the reek of alcohol and tobacco on his breath.

"People may talk," she whispered.

"Let them talk," he said, taking a step closer to her. His hands moved to her upper arms.

That was when the man crossed the street. He went from a stroll to a jog, as if trying to beat the nonexistent traffic, and stepped onto the sidewalk just behind Voigt. Marta's expression changed as she looked at the man, and Voigt half-turned to see what had captured her attention, but the gun was low enough that neither of them saw it before the muzzle flash lit up the storefront behind them.

Two shots. Voigt fell hard against her, the hands on her arms suddenly becoming anchors. A third shot exploded Voigt's head, splashing warm blood across Marta's cheeks and chin. She looked into the shooter's eyes and recognized him as another employee from work. His name was Peter something, and he had been let go a few days earlier, accused of theft. He was crying now as he finally saw her. He knew that she recognized him, that she could identify him to the police. He brought the gun up again.

Two more shots. This time Marta did fall, tripping over her own feet, Voigt's dead weight against her chest like a boulder. He pressed the air out of her when she hit the pavement and she coughed, staring up at the clouds as Peter stepped over them and began to run. She coughed and everything in her entire torso ached. His footsteps echoed. The sky overhead seemed like a bowl which was placed over her head, so impossibly close that she expected the rooftops nearby to press against the firmament, dimpling it around the stars. It was so hard to breathe.

A new face appeared above hers. Smooth, unblemished, looking more like a boy than the adult woman Marta knew it was. She wore wire-rimmed glasses under the brim of a pageboy cap, and her mouth was set in a firm, determined line.

"Are you alive?"

Marta coughed in response. There was blood on her lips.

This was the only confirmation the other woman needed. She grabbed Voigt by the shoulders and roughly hauled him to one side as if he was a sack of potatoes. Marta was grateful for the relief of having him off of her and tried to take a deep breath. That sent another explosion of pain through her whole body. She trembled and closed her eyes as Timo stepped over her, one foot on either side, bent in half with both hands on her hips like a scolding teacher.

"Do I have to carry dead weight?" Timo hissed.

Marta only coughed again. Timo sighed and pressed something against Marta's chest. "Hold that here. You've already lost much blood."

Marta blacked out. Her next memory was being half-dragged down the street with Timo's voice in her ear. She was singing some drinking song, slurring her words, letting anyone who saw them think they were a couple of drunks on their way home after a bender. She tried to add her own voice but lacked the breath to do more than wheeze.

Somehow she made it to the backseat of a car. Timo climbed in on top of her like a sweaty prom date, pawing at Marta's clothes until she exposed the wounds. Marta let herself sink into the upholstery, eyes closed, head swimming. Her body was strangely light, and she wondered why Timo had such a hard time carrying her. Her eyes wouldn't focus, but she could see the material on the car's roof was sagging and full of holes.

"No doctors," Timo said, and Marta wondered if she had asked for one. Everything was just so strange. Timo continued her speech as she worked. She sounded out of breath, adding to the image of teenagers fooling around. Maybe Timo was reminding herself of who they were, of why the logical solution was not possible for them. "Doctors means questions about what happened tonight. Right now it's clean, if not exactly tidy."

Unless the shooter tells someone Voigt had been with a woman. But she was still lucid enough to think through that possibility and realize Timo had probably ensured the shooter wouldn't be around to give his version to anyone. What had his name been? Peter. She remembered him from the office. Black line of sweat around his collar, sickly complexion, very thin hair on top. It was getting harder to breathe but she managed to wheeze out four words.

"I'm going... to die."

Timo said, "Marta Gresham is already dead, darling. She died back there on that street corner and she'll disappear in some morgue. An unfortunate who will end up in a pauper's grave. But you... there's hope for you." She put a hand on the uninjured shoulder and lined up their faces. "Are you still with me?"

Her eyes swam. Marta was dead. That meant she was herself again. She was... her name. She couldn't remember her name. But there was another name, a word she used because using her real name in public was dangerous.

"Circe."

"That's right," Timo said. "That's your name for right now. I'm going to leave you here so I can drive us somewhere safe, okay?"

She climbed out of the backseat without waiting for an answer. The woman who had spent three years answering to a name that wasn't her own reached up to touch her now-bandaged wounds. It still hurt like fire, but maybe it was a little better. Or maybe she was dying and the relief was just proof that Heaven existed. She closed her eyes and grunted as the car moved and made her rock against the seat.

Circe wasn't her name. It was just her codename, what her bosses used to identify her without compromising her safety. She calmed her mind and accepted Marta was dead. The carefully crafted person she had helped invent was no more, and she could let go of so many false memories and lies. It was like scraping ice from a window and suddenly seeing the world clearly again.

"Cassiane." She said her own name like a prayer, the first time in ages she had dared to say those three syllables out loud. It was like a song she'd loved but forgotten, and she smiled as she wrapped herself up in the sound. "My name is Cassiane Jurick..."

Her body suddenly became completely weightless, as if she was untethered from the Earth and gravity. It was like she was on a plane which had suddenly gone into a nosedive. She was airborne, levitating, flying, and she didn't know how to get back to her body. As she floated, she became aware of her mind turning dark as well. She didn't know if drifting off would mean she risked never waking up, but at the moment it was just too hard to hold onto consciousness. If she did pass away, at the very least she could take comfort in knowing she died as herself. She imagined herself high above the city looking down at its mazes of streets, the slate rooftops.

And there, just to the north of where Timo was driving, she saw the Wall. It was the edge of a knife cutting through the city like a blade slicing through muscle. It was the bullet, alien and wrong burrowing deeper into her flesh. She looked down on it and saw the two halves of the city spreading out on either side, the blood seeping from her body into the upholstery of the backseat.

The vision faded and the woman who was Circe, who had been Marta, who had again become Cassiane, felt herself drifting into space, farther away from the body bleeding in the back of the car.

CHAPTER ONE

THERE WERE ghost stations in Berlin on this side of the Wall. Passing through one was like slipping into a particularly eerie dream. Trains slowed to a crawl as they passed through dimly-lit stations populated only by heavily-armed East German soldiers. No one was allowed to leave the train in these stations even if there was a technical difficulty. Any kind of photography was forbidden. Passengers could see the stairs leading up to the surface were bricked over, along with torn and faded adverts which hadn't been changed since the Wall was erected in 1961.

Only a handful of these stations existed. They were heavily guarded, well-documented, and impossible to breach.

All except for one.

Regenstrasse was a slum of a street, long forgotten and ignored by those in power. Dusty windows stared out from abandoned storefronts like blind eyes, and trash gathered on street curbs. The subway station closed years before the Wall was erected, the entrance barred and quickly fading to invisibility by those unfortunate enough to call this place home. Transit officials left the station off the map of their routes and, soon, it was as if the cramped space never even existed.

Timothea Riddock had no idea who originally discovered their station, or how, but it was a godsend. Safe from the prying eyes of soldiers and random searches which would endanger any aboveground safehouse, it was the perfect place to regroup after the shooting. Gaining access was not easy under ordinary circumstances, and doing it while weighted down with Circe's dead weight presented an enormous challenge.

Access was gained by first going to a psychiatrist whose office was located on the ground floor of a neglected building. The office was at the back of the lobby, under the stairs, easy to ignore even by people who worked upstairs. There were enough tenants in the building to provide cover for them - a dentist, a lawyer, a chiropractor - but most of the commercial spaces had been empty for as long as Timo had been masquerading as Dr. Minna Lippert.

The therapy office was surrounded by vacancies on all sides but Timo was still grateful it was after-hours when she brought Circe into the building. She was stronger than she looked but dead weight was impossible to move without making a ruckus. By the time she muscled the uncooperative woman into the office and shut the door behind them, she was breathless and sweating. She put Circe on the couch as gently as possible, which wasn't very gentle at all, and slumped against the wall to catch her breath.

"What a night," she muttered.

She had been watching Circe and Voigt on their date. It was standard surveillance, recording what she could without getting so close that she might be noticed. She saw the assassin approaching and was out of her car before the first bullet hit Voigt, and her own weapon was drawn by the time Circe hit the ground. The assassin ducked and ran, stopped short when he saw Timo in his path. She saw his eyes widen in the flash of her pistol just before they were obscured by a puff of blood from the new hole in his forehead.

The police had most likely already found both bodies. She didn't care what story they concocted to explain what happened. Her job was to ensure Marta Gresham was not part of the narrative, and she'd succeeded at that. Now she just had to get the operative to the station where she could treat the wounds properly and she could recover.

The filing cabinet in the corner was pulled out, the edge of the carpet lifted, and a trap door opened to reveal a ladder into the basement. Timo managed to descend with Circe over her shoulder like a bag of flour, grunting and heaving with the effort. Going down a ladder one-handed was difficult enough without a whole second person's weight to contend with, but it still only took her a handful of minutes even with Circe's limp body draped over her shoulder like a rucksack. She ached and was dripping sweat when she finally reached the bottom, but the pain would only last a few moments. She could withstand a few moments of practically any discomfort.

One section of the basement was bricked off from prying eyes of plumbers and other servicemen. Only Timo had the key to this area, and she used it to gain access to a spiral metal staircase which led down into an all-consuming darkness. At the bottom of the stairs was a doorway which led into their true base of operations in this part of the world: their ghost station.

The room was mostly square, narrower near the door and very gradually widening at the opposite end of the space. At one time it had been heavily trafficked by commuters on their way to work in Berlin, but twin walls of pale yellow brick blocked off the stairs on one side and the train tracks at the other. The ceiling was elegantly vaulted, and three caged light bulbs hung down like spiders mated with fireflies. They swayed gently with the motion of a train which had just passed, the echo of its roar still echoing off the cracked floor tiles. She knew the train well; it was the closest the outside world ever came to intruding on this safe haven. No natural light reached the station, and the only fresh air came from the thinnest of vents at the top of the wall.

Timo knew the space well enough that she could traverse it with the lights off, not that there were many obstacles in her way: a bed against one wall and a desk against the other. Two chairs. A bag of supplies tucked in one corner. Rifles propped up against the wall next to the bed.

Timo deposited Circe on the bed and proceeded to check her wounds, making sure they hadn't reopened due to being carted around like a bag of flour. She redressed the damage, this time using a proper first-aid kit. Her Aunt Vera had been a medical doctor who taught her everything she needed to know to survive the world. "You can't always count on a hospital being around. Sometimes you have to stitch yourself back together and get on with your day." The knowledge saved Vera's life in the Second World War, and helped Timo gain a spot in their Organization.

Once Circe was resting, Timo went to the desk and slumped wearily into the seat. She sighed, pressed two fingers against her forehead, and stared at the blank sheet of paper in front of her. Command would insist upon an update, but she couldn't even think of how to begin an account of such utter failure. Stanley Voigt was the director of a museum which housed several antiquities believed to have been stolen during the War. Circe was employed as his secretary with two goals. First, the one she completed very early in the mission, to confirm they were in possession of the stolen art. Second and most complex, to map out his supply line to find where the contraband came from.

Circe had been making great progress. Gaining his trust, learning the trade, and slowly gaining information on how art was being smuggled across the Wall. Timo was furious that all their hard work had amounted to nothing. With Voigt dead, his suppliers would find someone else to buy their goods. They couldn't get back into the museum to reclaim the items they knew were there without arousing suspicions.

If she had simply left Circe at the scene, perhaps paramedics would have arrived in time to save her life. But then she would have been in the hospital, the victim of a crime, subject to scrutiny by police and soldiers. The identity provided by the Organization was good but it wasn't perfect. She had to be taken off the board to protect every other mission, every other agent.

But damn, it wouldn't be easy to explain taking such a drastic move even if she knew it had been the right thing to do. She'd ruined three years of hard work and compromised their chances of ever getting the stolen artwork back to its rightful owners. That was all on her.

Timo looked over her shoulder at Circe. She looked like she was sleeping. Even the blood on her clothes looked like a floral design rather than anything critical. Timo left the desk and went back to the bed. She slipped her hand into Circe's and squeezed, ignoring the lack of response.

It was difficult not to think of her as Marta, even harder to think of her true name. For the past three years, Marta Gresham had come to Dr. Lippert's office every Tuesday and Thursday for her sessions. The hour spent in that office was the only time Circe didn't have to be on guard or vigilant about her surroundings. She would give her report, hand over any information she had gathered, and then they spent the rest of the hour simply talking. A few times, Circe took the opportunity to nap. She took off her shoes, stretched out on the couch, and fell asleep while Timo quietly encoded whatever information she'd been given.

Tonight, Timo had been wearing the armor of a handler from the moment she saw the gun. She was being professional. Circe was her agent, and she needed help. But now that they were ensconced snug in their tomb, the one tiny space in all of Berlin they could feel safe, the inner walls fell away and left only emotion. This was her friend, a woman she had shared many intimacies with over the past few years, and she was looking very, very pale. Her red hair was dark where it touched her face, which was dappled with beads of sweat. Timo took a clean rag and blotted away what she could.

"You are safe here, Cassiane," she whispered.

The unseen train was finally far enough away that the rattle had ceased and the world was still, the engine's sonorous grumble finally fading into an eerie silence. Timo imagined the rest of the world had disappeared with the sound. Its wars and its walls, the hatred and anger, secrets, lies. She put her head down, Circe's knuckles cold against her forehead, and closed her eyes. She didn't believe in a deity so she didn't pray, but she sent every good thought and all the healing energy that might be swirling around into the woman she considered her only true friend.

Timo finally wrote, encoded, and sent off the update. It went out as standard post, which they'd found safer than trying to sneak correspondence out of the country. The body of the letter looked mundane enough to an outsider, even someone who might be looking for secret communiques, and the cipher was complex enough that no one could break it even if they suspected a hidden message. This method meant they would have to wait a very long time for a response. Fortunately this was a rare time when they could afford to wait.

Circe didn't wake again until the morning after the shooting. Timo was dozing next to the bed and startled awake at the sound of her name being weakly spoken. She sat up straighter and tightened her grip on Circe's hand.

"You are awake," she said, her voice rough from exhaustion.

"I'm alive." Circe looked away from Timo and let her gaze drift through the room.

Timo said, "You're probably very weak. Tired. You can rest."

"Voigt?"

"Dead. I haven't had a chance to get the newspaper yet, but there was little doubt. I eliminated the gunman. The police will most likely consider it open-and-shut. Did you recognize him?"

Circe said, "A man from work. A lay-about. Completely useless. Voigt fired him last week. I assume this was retribution." She closed her eyes and relaxed against the bedding, her lips twisting to show her teeth. "Everything hurts."

"I wasn't exactly gentle with you. It was difficult bringing you here."

"I'm sure. Thank you, Timo."

"It's my job to keep you safe. And you're very welcome, Cassiane." She paused. "I've sent word back to Command about what happened. We should hear back from them soon. I predict they will send instructions for our extraction. In the meantime, you will heal."

Circe twisted her lips into an expression of dissatisfaction and looked away.

"What is it?"

"I failed. Everything we've done over the past three years was for nothing."

Timo said, "That was always a possibility. Command could have aborted the mission at any time, for whatever reason. You could have been discovered and forced to flee. This outcome was not your fault. And the important thing is that you survived. Voigt may be gone, but I'm certain he has a successor who will use whatever system and routes are already in place. Something can be salvaged."

"I hope you're right."

"Right or wrong, it's not your problem to solve right now." She brushed the hair away from Circe's forehead and let her hand rest there briefly to check her temperature. "Do you need anything? Water?"

"Sleep, I think..."

"That's reasonable. I'll be here if you need anything else. Rest." She stood up to kiss Circe's cheek, then shifted her aim to press her lips to Circe's mouth. "I am very glad you're okay, Cassiane."

"Thank you for saving me, Timothea."

Timo kissed her again and slipped her hand away from Circe's grip.

Over the next few days, with supplies pilfered from medical offices in the building above, the station transformed into a hospital room. Circe slowly regained her strength and soon complained of being confined to the bed. Timo tried to distract her with board games and coloring books - there wasn't much worth stealing in the waiting rooms of their fellow tenants, so she made do with what they had. Circe griped about being treated like a child or, even worse, an invalid.

"Even if you were healthy enough to go wandering around the city, Voigt's death is still too fresh. We can't risk someone from the museum seeing his secretary suddenly alive and well at the market. We will receive word from the Organization soon. Until then, we will wait."

Circe used the crayons and slips of paper to make a set of playing cards. She taught Timo how to play poker, Timo taught Circe how to play Kings in the Corner. They were used to only seeing each other an hour at a time, twice a week, so at first there was a certain thrill to spending more time together. But they eventually grew irritated by one another.

It was Timo's responsibility to take their laundry out "into the world," wash it, and bring it back. All chores that involved leaving their safe space fell to her. Grocery shopping was a particular pain, seeing as it required taking from a stockpile of money which was rapidly dwindling. Tensions became frayed and long silences were broken by sharp words and shouting matches that only stopped when they realized they risked discovery. One morning, both of them in especially sour moods, Timo made a comment about Circe sitting in her parlor waiting for the maid to return with her evening meal.

"You can't imagine I prefer this." Circe was sitting on the bed in her undershirt, a fresh bandage over the quickly-healing wound in her chest. "At least you get to go outside. Breathe fresh air, see other people. I would love to do one of these errands you find so tedious. While I sit here, staring at nothing but bland on bland on *bland*. I am so sick of looking at everything in this blasted room!"

Timo was angrily depositing folded laundry into the milk crate that served as Circe's wardrobe. "I am sorry you find my appearance so mundane."

Circe grimaced at that; she clearly hadn't intended insult. "Anyone looks mundane after weeks of monotony."

"You wouldn't like it much out there," Timo said. "You can feel their eyes on you everywhere. That fucking wall... I can feel it. Even when I can't see it, I know it's there. Looming. It might as well be thirty meters high. Men with guns who would kill me if they had even an inkling of who I am." She waved off that thought. "No. No, they would not make it that easy. If they suspected who I was, they would know about you. They would torture me for information. But yes, Cassiane, the picnics in the park every Sunday are *so lovely* and I've become quite good at flying kites."

Timo kicked the empty laundry bag away and stalked toward the far wall, hands on her hips. She looked like an angry bull. Circe felt a pang of regret and looked away from her. Silence spread from the both of them until it filled the room like a gas. Timo looked down and saw the bag which had toppled over when the laundry hit it.

"Oh... I forgot about these," she said, her voice quiet and almost apologetic. "I brought you more puzzle books. English and German."

"Thank you," Circe said, her voice equally small. "I'm sorry."

Timo waved off the apology but didn't look at her. Circe stood up and crossed the room until she was standing behind her, Timo's face to the wall. Timo reached up and wiped at her face and Circe's guilt ratcheted up a few more levels. She placed one hand on Timo's shoulder and squeezed, trying to find the right thing to say. Timo hesitated and then covered Circe's hand with her own. They stood like that for a long time, neither was sure how long, and Circe still couldn't think of anything to say. Finally, she settled on revealing a fact she had recently become aware of.

"There's no reason for you to be here."

"I thought you might appreciate the company." Timo sounded equal parts distraught and annoyed.

"No, I... That isn't what I meant." She put her other hand on Timo's other shoulder. "There's no reason you can't lock up the office every night at the end of business hours, go to your apartment at a reasonable time. In fact, it might even benefit your cover if you did that. But you stay here."

"You would be alone otherwise," Timo said.

Circe turned Timo around and put both hands back on her shoulders. "I am very grateful for your company, Timothea."

Timo pressed her lips together and swallowed hard, eyes wide and unblinking. Circe had thought they were brown but, this close, she could see they were flecked with a curious shade of green.

"I never thanked you for saving my life."

"It's my job."

Circe shrugged. "But regardless... heroes are generally rewarded with a kiss."

There was a moment - either when Circe leaned in, or as she was wetting her lips with a deliberate sweep of her tongue - when Timo could have stopped it. Turning her head, whispering a refusal, or simply putting her hands on Circe's hips and pushing her away, but instead she tilted her head and accepted the kiss. She exhaled like someone who had been holding their breath, and Circe stepped even closer to her. The kiss was everything she'd spent years telling herself not to want. It was every sinful thought, every wrong urge, and it was being handed to her by the worst possible person. But she accepted it eagerly. Her tongue found Circe's teeth, and one hand alighted on Circe's chest, fingers curling in the rough cotton of her tank top.

Circe broke the kiss by changing the angle of her head, keeping her lips close enough for Timo to feel the words "is this okay?" as much as hear them.

Timo closed her eyes, hating that the option was being given to her. She pressed her lips to Circe's jaw and moved her hand up, over her neck, into her short hair, and grabbed a handful of it.

"I don't know if it's okay," Timo finally said, "but I want it."

Circe pulled Timo away from the wall and walked her toward the bed. Timo allowed herself to be guided, her mind battling with the logistics of what was about to happen and the wisdom of engaging in physical activity given Circe's still-healing wound. But all of that was just a dull whisper compared to the overwhelming focus she had on the kiss. She'd kissed men before, or rather been kissed by men before, and she'd never seen the appeal. She'd never felt the urge to continue it. But now she never wanted to stop. If this was a kiss, if this is what all those men were seeking, then perhaps she could forgive them for being a little eager in their pursuits.

They reached the bed. Circe moved her hands to Timo's suspenders and hooked her fingers underneath them.

"Sit," Circe said.

Timo gripped Circe's wrists. "Have you ever done this before?"

Circe nodded. "I have."

Timo turned them both so that Circe's legs were pressing against the mattress. She pushed back and Circe dropped into a sitting position, face frozen in surprise.

"Then I have been waiting for this much longer than you have. You will wait your turn."

Circe blinked in surprise. The corners of her mouth rose slightly. "So aggressive, Miss Riddock." She let her hands fall. "Do with me as you will."

Timo's assertiveness wavered as she realized she had no plan beyond that moment. She wet her lips and dropped to her knees, and Circe leaned back to expose her midsection. Timo unfastened the belt, brow furrowed as if the task was immensely complex. Circe shifted her weight so her pants and underwear could be dragged down.

"Do you know what you're doing down there?"

"I believe I can... ah..."

She pressed her lips together and bent down. She was worried about her glasses getting in the way but that was only a passing concern. Circe pushed her hands into Timo's hair and held tightly, making her focus on the task. She started slow and timid, her tongue barely past her lips with her teeth getting in the way, but she soon became bolder. It was the same way she felt the first time she drove a car. It was the feeling of power, of being where she belonged.

Timo put one hand on Circe's thigh and pushed it gently as she brought her other hand up. She moved her mouth long enough to rub her fingers against Circe's wet folds, then looked up to see the other woman's reaction. Circe's eyes were closed, her lips parted, face and chest flush. Timo stared at her as she used her fingers to finish what her tongue started. When she moved her thumb to the small bud above the folds, she saw something amazing.

She saw Cassiane Jurick's true face.

It wasn't Circe, it wasn't Marta Gresham or any of the other identities the woman may have worn in the past. Timo suddenly knew she was seeing the real person, the girl who had grown up to be an assassin and spy. It was so startling that her fingers stopped moving, and Cassiane responded with a low growl and reached to grab Timo's hand.

"Don't stop. I'm almost..."

Timo resumed. She bent down and moved her thumb so she could use her tongue instead, and Cassiane's hips came off the bed so sharply that Timo's glasses were finally knocked askew. She didn't take the time to fix them as she could tell the end was near. She didn't let up until the tension went out of Cassiane's body, until the hand in her hair went limp, and the body above her slumped backward onto the mattress.

She wiped the back of her hand over her mouth and sat up. Cassiane's chest rose and fell with her breathing, then stood and turned away.

"Come here."

Timo shook her head, looking down at her hand as if it was a foreign object.

"Timothea," Cassiane said with more force. "Come to bed."

"I can't."

Cassiane sighed. "Goddamn it." The bed protested as she sat up. "I wish I could fucking smoke in here."

"There's barely any ventilation. Ignore the smell, we would asphyxiate."

"I just want a damn cigarette."

Timo went to the desk and yanked the jacket off the back of the chair. She hurled it in Cassiane's direction. "Go, then! Go up on the street and smoke and let the police see your face. Maybe they'll let you have another one before they put a fucking bullet in your head!"

Cassiane glared at her and Timo cursed under her breath, grabbing a handful of her hair in frustration. She was shaking, and nervous energy made her pace in front of the desk. All she could hear was the loud huffing of her breath, the scuff of her shoes on the hard ground.

"I've never... done what we just did."

"You hinted at that." Cassiane tilted her head to the side. "Unless you mean... You mean you've never done that with another woman, yes?"

Timo didn't answer, didn't look at her.

"Aha. I see." She folded the jacket and tossed it onto the pillow. "Come here, Timothea."

"I don't know."

Cassiane's voice was gentle now. "Please."

Timo walked to the bed and sat down. Cassiane shifted to face her, one arm around Timo's waist and the other on her thigh. Timo kept her eyes down, focusing on her knees and the floor beyond them. When she finally looked up, she saw Cassiane staring at her.

"Let me guess what's going through your head right now, yeah? The way you kissed me, it was like you understood something. So I think every kiss you had before that one was lacking. I don't think it had anything to do with me personally." Her hand moved higher. Timo's breath caught and she tried to conceal it by breathing slower. "I don't think you ever considered... what just happened. And when I presented it as a possibility, your eyes were opened. And now you're scared. You're worried about what it would mean."

Timo whispered, "I don't want to be... one of those..."

"Because it sickens you?"

"Because of..." She nodded toward the entrance. "Them. What they would think. What they would do if they believed I was..." She flinched. "Woman, bad enough. Greek, even worse. I don't need to give them another reason to throw me in the dirt."

Cassiane said, "Then it doesn't have to mean anything. It just has to be something that happens, right here in this room, between you and I. Just like everything else in this room. It doesn't affect the outside world because it doesn't exist. This is a place where I am myself, where you can take off all your masks. It is the only place within a thousand miles where I can hear my name being spoken without breaking into a cold sweat."

She squeezed Timo's thigh.

"Or. I could put my pants back on. And we can play cards. The choice is yours."

Timo moved her gaze to see Cassiane's hand. After a long, slow deliberation where she was fairly sure no coherent thoughts actually passed through her mind, she moved her hand to the fly of her pants, unzipped it, and wrapped her fingers around Cassiane's. Neither of them spoke. Cassiane adjusted her position, moving her arm so she could hold her hand flat. Timo gasped and went stiff.

"Okay...?"

"Mm-hmm." Eyes closed, red blooming on her cheeks, tongue sneaking out to brush across her lips as she anticipated what was next.

Cassiane bent down and began kissing Timo's throat. Timo closed her eyes and spread her legs, moving her hips. The bed squeaked underneath them, and her toes curled in her boots. Cassiane's tongue found her earlobe, slid down to the collar of her shirt, and sucked on the smooth skin in between. Her free hand came up to tickle the short hair at the nape of Timo's neck, causing her to shudder violently and then moan, loud and slow.

She didn't know if she would be able to hold back, didn't even want to try. She whispered, "Cassiane, please," and then felt what an orgasm was supposed to be. It was nothing like the thing she felt under her own touch, or with her own bedding bundled between her legs. This was something spiritual and real and absolutely amazing. She put her hand on top of Cassiane's, the thick material of her trousers between them, and convulsed with the force of what had just happened. She heard Cassiane's laugh, low and throaty, next to her ear.

"Good god."

"Just don't fall in love with me, Miss Riddock," Cassiane said, freeing her hand. "Rookie mistake, and not something that would help our situation."

Timo flopped backward. After a moment, Cassiane lay down next to her. They both stared up at the vaulted ceiling of their little tomb. Finally Timo broke the silence.

"All this time we've been wasting on fucking card games..."

Cassiane laughed and slapped the back of her hand against Timo's stomach.

CHAPTER TWO

SOME MORNINGS, Timo sat in the therapy office and stared at the fogged glass of the door. She had to wait until the building was quiet before she risked leaving. She didn't want her neighbors to notice how long she seemed to spend at work. One man, a dentist with an office on the second floor, had once seen her coming into the building with laundry and joked that it would make sense that she lived there. "I don't think I've ever actually seen you leave." She'd laughed off the comment but kept an eye on him. If he was truly suspicious, he would have to be dealt with.

This time, however, her hesitation had nothing to do with strategy. She delayed because opening the door meant returning to reality. A world where she had responsibilities and where dangerous men lurked with truncheons and laws meant to punish people like her. After two weeks spent sharing Cassiane's bed, she could no longer deny the type of woman she was. So she sat in her chair and stared at the door. She was dressed in her casual clothes - a wool blazer, a peach blouse, a skirt past her knees - but she'd spent much of the past two weeks naked. Her hair was neatly styled, but she wanted it to be mussed and tangled by Cassiane's fingers.

Eventually she couldn't put off her mission any longer. They needed food. She gathered her things and left the office, moved quickly through the lobby, and made it to the street without encountering any other tenants.

Timo did her shopping all over the city to avoid any grocers noticing she bought enough for two people. Everyone she did business with seemed friendly enough, but there was no telling who might be an informant. She turned up the collar of her coat, tucked her scarf into the opening, and kept her head down to avoid making eye contact with the other similarly guarded people shuffling through the aisles.

She was examining an apple for bruising when she became aware of a presence to her right. Her first instinct was to step away and casually establish some distance, but he spoke before she could move.

"You are to remain."

Timo went very still. She faced forward. The man was only a blur of his charcoal gray coat and a flash of red beard. He spoke German with a vague accent she couldn't identify.

"There is a need," he continued, "and KYP is unable to get another team in place. It is quite fortunate that your mission was scrubbed and you have become available."

"What is required?" She picked up another apple and squeezed.

"Not for me to say." He rearranged some oranges. "I am only delivering the message that you and the operative are to remain where you are. Await further instructions."

She had more questions but knew he wouldn't provide answers even if he had them. He stepped away and, when she finally left the produce section, she saw no hint of a man with a dark coat or a big red beard. She finished her shopping, paid, and went back to the office without breaking into a run or appearing to be in a hurry. The lobby was again empty, fortunate, but she could hear people on the stairs. She moved quickly to the sanctuary of her office and then began the descent into the only safe place in all of Germany.

Cassiane was waiting on the bed, legs folded in front of her, hunched over a newspaper spread out on the mattress in front of her. She wore her undershirt and a pair of underwear, nothing else. Timo was briefly distracted by the curve of her calf and the lines of her stomach.

"We have orders."

Cassiane sat up straight, eyes wide, shoulders squared. "About damn time."

"You won't like it." Timo put the groceries down and turned to face her. "We are to remain where we are and await a mission."

"What the hell have we been doing?"

Timo said, "I thought we were waiting on permission to get the hell out of here. But it would seem they need us for something else."

Cassiane cursed in Greek and grabbed the paper with both hands. She hurled it, the pages flapping like the wings of an angry crow before drifting to the ground.

"And I am supposed to remain hidden while we wait? I cannot bear this imprisonment any longer. As lovely and distracting as your presence has been, I feel the walls getting closer every day." She put a hand against her throat as if clawing at a choker. "I need fresh air, Timo. You can't understand what it is like to be locked away like this. Surely the danger must have passed by now. Voigt's death must be long forgotten compared to the other atrocities I'm sure are being committed throughout the city."

Timo came closer to the bed, chewing her bottom lip. She pushed aside the strap of Cassiane's undershirt and peeled away the bandage to check the progress of her healing.

"We'll go for a walk tonight."

Cassiane's face remained impassive. "You say that now. But if you are spooked, or you decide between then and now~"

"No. You have my word. You've been hidden long enough." She reached up and fingered the long stands of Cassiane's hair. "But perhaps a haircut would be prudent..."

Cassiane put her arms around Timo and gripped her upper thighs with both hands, pulling her forward. Timo dropped her hands to Cassiane's shoulders and, forced to choose between straddling and sitting, opted to bend her knees and settle on the other woman's lap.

"I believe you simply want to see how I look with shorter hair."

Timo shook her head. "It is all for the mission, I assure you."

Cassiane laughed and pressed her lips to the front of Timo's shirt. Though they had spent the morning in bed, Timo decided they had nothing better to do at the moment, and started unbuttoning the shirt to give Cassiane better access.

Cassiane was going mad. Timo patiently explained the routine, and why they had to wait, so she knew logically why they couldn't just run upstairs. The other tenants in the building went home between five and six o'clock. An hour after that, the cleaning crews arrived and began roaming the halls. Their work took anywhere from ninety minutes to two hours.

"So we leave before the cleaners arrive!"

"And risk being caught when we come back inside after hours." Timo checked her watch. "We don't have much longer. Sit down. You're making me anxious."

Cassiane grumbled and resumed pacing. She touched the nape of her neck, which felt naked and exposed after the haircut Timo gave her that afternoon. She'd also used coffee grounds to darken its color, and the smell hovered around her head like gnats. Still, it was a good disguise, and she'd been surprised by how slow and intimate the process had been. First, Timo washed her hair and then carefully brushed out every tangle like it was a religious rite. When Timo's fingers lightly touched the shell of her ear, Cassiane flashed back to her biting it. The same when she brushed trimmings from the nape of Cassiane's neck.

They decided on keeping the hair chin-length rather than mimicking Timo's own mop. Timo thought they would draw more attention if they both looked masculine, and Cassiane had to agree. She couldn't necessarily say the change was for the better, but it was definitely something she could get used to. The cut felt symbolic. Her veil had finally been lifted, literally and figuratively. She touched it again as she pivoted on the ball of her foot and began another circuit of the room.

"Okay," Timo sighed, "the sun is definitely down and the building is empty. Let's go."

Cassiane clapped her hands together. Timo led the way out, but Cassiane crowded behind with her hands on Timo's shoulders. She squeezed, unable to hide her excitement, and she thought she could see Timo's cheeks lift in a smile when she glanced back over her shoulder.

"Do not scratch me with your claws."

"I never scratch you," Cassiane said.

"I have the markings to prove otherwise."

Cassiane dragged the back of one hand down Timo's shoulder in apology, then tightly squeezed her bicep through the sleeve of her shirt.

"Thank you, Timothea."

"You were right. It's time. You have been locked away long enough."

The ground floor was abandoned, as promised, but a security light still burning at either end of the lobby cast a pale, ghostly glow over the gray walls. Cassiane slid her hand down Timo's arm until their hands met, fingers automatically locking into a tight grip. Her impatience had given away to anxiety, nerves, fear. The walls she'd considered stifling moments ago were now security, protection. Cassiane steeled herself and let Timo lead her out into the cold night.

Fresh air. Timo kept walking once they were outside but Cassiane stopped in the doorway. Their hands slipped apart as she tilted her head back, eyes closed, and let the wind push against her. She took a deep breath and let it out. She could hear people in the distance. When she opened her eyes, she could see the clouds high above, and a thin ribbon of her breath twisted and danced up to join it. For the first time since her "murder," she felt as if she had actually survived.

Timo had stopped not far away, hands in her pockets, waiting for the spell to end. Cassiane finally looked at her and smiled.

"Thank you for letting me come up here."

"You're welcome," Timo said softly. "I'm sorry I kept you down there for so long, but if anyone had seen you or recognized..." She caught herself, obviously aware she was falling back into an old argument. After a moment, she repeated, "You are welcome. Now, where do you want to go?"

Cassiane hadn't thought that far ahead. She barely remembered the neighborhood. Her visits had always been business-related, and she was always more focused on the task at hand. Were there restaurants nearby? If so, were any of them still open? Timo obviously sensed her unease and took pity.

"Come with me. I will take you back to my apartment."

"Your apartment?"

Timo shrugged. "It's not much. But I have a little food, and better facilities than you are accustomed to. You can take a bath if you wish."

Cassiane was already moving. She took Timo's hand again. "Hurry," she said.

"You don't know the way!"

"Then show me!"

Timo laughed and let herself be pulled along. For a moment, they were simply two women out late, enjoying each other's company with no worries in the world.

Timo's apartment was actually smaller than the station, but a four-paned window above the sink made all the difference. Cassiane went straight to it, hands flat on the counter, and leaned in close to the glass so she could look down the street. She saw other windows lit from within, pale yellow lamplight and the flickering glow of television screens. Timo had continued into the apartment by pulling aside a curtain which separated the kitchen and dining room from her bedroom. Timo tossed her coat onto the unmade bed and quickly gathered a few scattered pieces of dirty laundry.

"You can find something to eat in the cabinet to your right," she said. "I keep most of the groceries I buy in the station, but I think you can find something to snack on."

Cassiane opened the cabinet and took out a bag of graham crackers. "Milk?"

"Icebox."

She got the bottle and brought it into the bedroom. Timo had taken a seat on the foot of the bed, and Cassiane joined her. She couldn't explain how it felt to be out of her cell. It was as if she could feel all the people around her, the hum of lives being lived on the other side of the wall. Footsteps from above thudded across the ceiling. Someone outside blared their car horn. She closed her eyes and tilted her head to one side so she wouldn't miss any of it.

"Thank you for bringing me outside."

"You were right," Timo said. "It's time. I haven't fully appreciated what it was like for you to be trapped down there." She put her hand on the back of Cassiane's neck and traced wide circles with her fingernails. Cassiane shuddered and swayed. "I think it's been long enough. And you look different enough now. Maybe you can start pulling your weight with the groceries."

Cassiane opened her eyes to look at her. "Yes?"

Timo nodded. "If we have to stay here and wait for further instructions, there's no reason to keep you in a box."

"Then I must thank you again." She leaned in to kiss Timo but stopped herself, turning to look at the bed. It was narrow, but she had a feeling they could make it work. "Do I have time to thank you properly before we have to go back?"

"No point in going back tonight. We'll sneak back in tomorrow morning." She moved her hands to the top button of Cassiane's shirt. "I've often fantasized about having you in this room. I have a very detailed script about what is about to happen."

Cassiane pushed Timo down onto the mattress. "Let me know if I leave anything out," she said as she climbed on top of her.

CHAPTER THREE

THEY HAD no papers or story to support a new identity, but Cassiane also couldn't present herself as Marta Gresham while in public. The poor secretary had been declared dead weeks ago even without the benefit of a body. It was also impossible for her to use her true identity, as Cassiane Jurick would most likely be arrested on sight for being an enemy agent. But now that they'd "broken the seal," it would be cruel to force her back into the cage all day every day. So Timo used her rudimentary skills to create a set of new identification for someone named Sophie Rasch, who would take the position of Timo's secretary.

"Always the receptionist," Cassiane grunted.

"It's an easy enough job, since you already have the skills for it, and people tend to overlook the person working the front desk." She folded her arms. "Not to mention the fact you should be thanking your lucky stars for anything that gets you aboveground."

Cassiane acknowledged that with a dip of her chin.

They'd been going through the motions of their new cover story for almost two work weeks, eight days all told. Timo even saw a few patients, people who found her despite a lack of advertising or word of mouth and made appointments. She didn't know how much good she was doing them, but at the very least she could say she wasn't doing them harm. On the weekends, Cassiane went to Timo's apartment where they shared her bed.

On Thursday morning, they arrived to find someone sitting on the floor outside their locked office. She was young, perhaps a teenager. Her hair was blonde, and she was buried under at least three layers of warm clothing. Her head was bent forward to read the book in laying open in her lap. Cassiane slipped one hand under her jacket to touch the butt of her revolver as Timo cautiously approached the stranger.

"*Hallo*," she said cautiously. "I'm Dr. Lippert. Can I help you?"

The girl looked up and Timo saw she was at least five years older than her original estimate. She smiled, closed her book on the strip of silk, and got to her feet with a flexibility that hinted at a gymnastic past. She brushed her center-parted hair out of her face and squared her shoulders. Her face was scrubbed and her blue eyes shone as she smiled.

"*Guten Morgen.* My name is Rosa Keller. I'm your eight o'clock appointment." She pushed up her sleeve to read the face of an oversized watch. "I admit I'm a little early. Habit. I am perfectly content to wait out here while you go about your business."

"That won't be necessary." Timo glanced at Cassiane for confirmation that she'd booked the appointment. Cassiane gave the smallest of nods, and Timo smiled at the girl again. Very few people in East Berlin could afford the luxury of a therapy session, which meant they didn't have to worry about many people seeking her out. But occasionally someone did appear, and it would look suspicious to turn them down. It also helped appearances if multiple people were seen coming and going from time to time. "Please, come inside. I'll just need a moment to settle in."

She unlocked the office door and led them in. Cassiane lagged behind so she could follow their guest inside and close the door behind them.

As soon as the latch clicked, the girl spoke in a much more confident voice. "I'm afraid I wasn't entirely truthful with you. I am your appointment, but my name is not Rosa Keller."

Cassiane slipped the gun from her pocket but kept it low by her hip.

"My name is Constance Grimaldi. I was sent by KYP to give you your new mission." She opened her book and withdrew a pressed sunflower. She pinched it by the stem and held it out. "For you."

"Thank God." Timo accepted the flower, a predetermined signal from their commanders. "It's about damned time you got here. I'm Timothea Riddock, that's Cassiane Jurick. Do you have any idea how long we've been waiting?"

Constance nodded and walked to the reception desk. "Yes, and I apologize. I had to travel from Turkey, and then travel arrangements had to be made so I could enter the country without raising suspicion. Our employers have not been idle, I assure you. What do you know about anthrax?"

"Brown powder," Timo said, "Don't touch it."

"Basically all you need to know." Constance put her book down and opened to a middle page so it could lay flat. She flipped five pages, then ripped out the sixth. She handed the page to Timo. "Now, what do you know of Pavel Rudin?"

Timo had to think for a moment. "Doesn't ring a bell."

Cassiane shook her head as well. She had remained by the door, just in case Constance's credentials or story didn't add up.

"His father was a scientist during World War II. Our side, back then. He followed in his papa's footsteps which means he's a Soviet now. We got word that he's here, in Berlin, to deliver a new strain of anthrax to people who intend to use it in some... widespread way. We don't have all the details but we know it's a large-scale attack."

Timo had taken the page from Constance's book into her office, leaving the door open so she could hear.

"That page has all the information we've gathered on Rudin. His appearance, where we believe he's staying, any known associates who may be in East Berlin providing him with help. We were very fortunate you were already here."

Cassiane said, "It didn't feel very fortunate."

"Yes," Constance said. "I heard you had been injured."

"She nearly died," Timo said from the other room.

Constance said, "I'm glad to see you're back on your feet."

"Timo... Timothea is a miracle worker," Cassiane said.

"So it would seem." Constance seemed at a loss for how to proceed, then finally cleared her throat and went to the office door. Cassiane followed. Timo was hunched over the desk, brushing the page with a compound which revealed small handwriting crammed into the margins. "The mission is to find Rudin, confirm he has the compound, and identify his buyers. Best case scenario, we eliminate him and the buyers and acquire the anthrax. Worst case, we have to destroy it."

"Worst case is they get suspicious and kill us," Timo said under her breath, too focused on her task to bother sounding concerned.

"Worst case while still constituting a success," Constance

corrected.

Timo nodded approvingly.

Constance said, "In the meantime, I'll be sticking around to lend you assistance on the mission."

"Thanks, but we can handle it," Cassiane said.

"You need me," Constance said. "Ideally we would have eight people working on this, but we couldn't exactly send in a whole squad. It was hard enough getting me here. Rudin is going to be on his guard. If he suspects he's under surveillance, he'll become a ghost. We have to be careful. I don't doubt your skills but I'm all the backup you're going to get."

Timo exchanged a look with Cassiane. Having someone else hanging around would be the death knell for their physical relationship, but she was right.

"Okay," Timo said. "The cover name you gave outside, it's secure?"

"Rosa Keller, photography student. I'm staying in the basement room of an elderly couple who live near here. They're known to us and sympathetic to the cause, so there shouldn't be any problems on that angle. As far as contact goes, I'll be a patient of Dr. Lippert. We'll meet for two hours on Tuesdays and Thursdays. That will also give us an excuse to be seen outside of the office. Emergency consultation, whatever." She looked at Cassiane. "What's your current cover story?"

"Dr. Lippert's receptionist. Sophie Rasch."

"That's good. It fits. A friendship grown during time spent in the waiting room." She nodded and then looked between the other two women. "I know you've been working together for a while. You've built a rapport. I don't want to get in the way of that. You know the lay of the land so I'll be deferring to Timothea as much as I can."

Timo said, "I appreciate that. And you can call me Timo."

Cassiane made a face at that, but didn't say anything. Constance was checking her watch and didn't notice. She looked up again with a smile.

"Now that all of that is taken care of, we should continue the pretense of a session. Just in case anyone is watching. It will give us a chance to get to know one another."

"Fantastic," Cassiane said.

Timo gestured at the wingback chairs. "Should we take a seat, like you're a real patient?"

Constance said, "Actually, I was curious about the ghost station where you kept Officer Jurick during her recuperation. It sounds absolutely marvelous."

Cassiane muttered, "Yes, it's a wonderland."

"Oh, I'm sure you're... I didn't mean..."

"It's fine." Cassiane waved off any apology and headed back out into the waiting room. "I'll keep up appearances out here. I'll buzz if anyone comes looking."

She left and closed the door on them before they could say anything. Her logical mind agreed that having extra hands would only be a benefit. Her emotional mind disagreed and was furious that now she'd have to share Timo with some stranger. She even hated the idea of sharing the nickname with someone else. She took a seat behind the desk and centered herself. She needed to be Sophie Rasch, receptionist, a woman going through a normal day at work with no need to be jealous or angry.

After a moment she steepled her fingers above the typewriter's keyboard, took a deep breath, and began typing up notes for nonexistent therapy sessions.

Constance led the way into the station, pausing on the threshold before continuing forward. Timo hesitated behind her in the shadows to watch her reaction. She'd spent so much time in the bolt-hole that she'd stopped truly seeing it. Instead of the cozy refuge, she saw a cramped brick cell with dirty clothes still bundled at the foot of a tiny metal bed, old containers of food which had somehow still attracted flies despite being underground and mostly sealed-off. There were old bandages tangled in a pile under the desk.

"Sorry for the mess."

"It's understandable." She was standing in the middle of the space, head tilted back to look at the ceiling dome above her. She walked the perimeter in silence for long minutes, the heels of her boots clicking on the tile floor. "I can't believe she spent weeks down here. I would go mad in just a few hours."

Timo leaned against the wall with her hands behind her back. "Yes, well, that's Circe for you. She compartmentalizes. She knew that she had to stay down here to save her life, so... that's what she did. She adapts to her situation. It's remarkable. I'm sure it's a big part of why she's been so successful in the field. Tell her to become Marta Gresham, that's who she is. Tell her she has to be Sophie Rasch, it's like a switch flips in her mind."

"Must make it hard to know if you've ever met the real person behind the mask."

"I don't presume I ever have," Timo said, although she knew that was a lie. She'd seen the real Cassiane Jurick many times. In pain, close to death, asleep, and in the throes of passion. She had no idea who Cassiane had been before coming to Berlin, before she joined the KYP and agreed to use names which weren't her own. But she had no doubt that she'd seen that long-suppressed woman several times in the past few weeks. More than that, Timo believe she knew that stranger very well.

"Why do you call her Circe?"

"It's her code name."

"I know that. But she called you Timothea, not Medea."

Timo shrugged. "The mask. As long as she's in enemy territory, the name is her armor."

Constance nodded her understanding, still examining the space. A train rumbled by, the sound slowly growing louder as the walls and floor trembled. Dust fell from the bricks, and everything in the station seemed suddenly alive and violent. Constance's eyes went wide until the train had passed and things became silent and still once more. She shook her head in disbelief.

"I'd have gone mad," she said again. She walked back to the doorway. "Let's go back upstairs."

Timo put a hand on Constance's arm to stop her. "Remember that when you deal with Circe. She's a woman who nearly died, who woke up here instead of Heaven, and was forced to stay here while she recuperated. When you look at her, you should be aware you're looking at a woman who not only survived this but found a way to thrive. *Verstehst du mich?*"

"Understood."

Timo let go of her arm and gestured for her to lead the way back to the surface.

While Timo and Constance were downstairs, Cassiane decided to take the opportunity to examine the file on their target. Pavel Rudin was staying only a few blocks away from Dr. Lippert's office on Regenstrasse. They'd most likely walked past the building numerous times without realizing its future importance in their lives. She read the description of Rudin but it was vague to the point of useless: black hair, beard, average height and weight. She could walk to the market and point out five Rudins in five minutes.

Their intelligence received word he was working on the new strain of anthrax at his home in Pushchino. When they discovered he was making travel arrangements to Berlin, they scrambled to ensure they would have a team there to observe him. Cassiane had wrinkled her nose when Constance called their botched mission 'fortunate,' but truthfully, she was glad that her injury would serve a greater purpose. She was returning the page to Timo's desk when they came back upstairs.

"I've memorized the information on Rudin," she said as Timo replaced the file cabinet. "The description is next to useless. We'll need a photograph."

"I can take care of that," Constance said. "I know what he looks like but I didn't want to risk being caught with a photo of him. I was going to stake out the place he's staying so I could take a new one, and provide it in the initial briefing. But I thought it was more important to meet the two of you first."

Timo said, "It was a smart call. He'll most likely be on his guard, so Circe and I will take shifts sitting with you. Less likely he'll notice anything amiss. You said we'll meet for two hours on Tuesdays and Thursdays?"

Constance nodded.

Cassiane said, "I've already added it to the calendar."

"You've been busy," Constance said.

"I learned how to fill time while I was recovering."

"I'm impressed." She looked at her watch. "We still have a lot of time to kill for our first 'session.' I can meet one of you tomorrow morning so we can watch Rudin's building."

Cassiane said, "I'll go first. Hopefully we'll get lucky and he'll poke his head out to get the newspaper and we won't have to waste much time just to get his face on film."

"Can't hurt to hope," Constance said, although she sounded skeptical.

Timo said, "There's a place nearby, the Perrot Café. You can meet there. Six o'clock?" Both women nodded their agreement. "Very good."

"And when this is over," Cassiane said, "what happens?"

Constance smiled. "When this is over, Miss Jurick, we all get the hell out of this godforsaken country and go the hell home."

CHAPTER FOUR

CASSIANE JURICK was born in Livadeia, Greece, youngest child of three. Her father was killed before she was born in an accident involving cattle which was never fully explained in her presence. "It's exactly how a man like him deserved to die," was the only thing her mother would say about the incident. She trusted her mother and never sought to learn about the man who sired her. She had two older sisters - a baker and a homemaker - who never left the country and seemed to have no ambitions to ever do so.

Cassiane was different. She remembered being at the beach as a child with an older woman. A friend of her mother, a neighbor, some random stranger who shared their blanket, she didn't recall. But when Cassiane pointed a chubby finger at the water and asked what was on the other side, the woman said, "Italy."

"What's Italy?"

"It's another country. Another language, new food, new culture, everything. You'll go one day. You'll see, it's beautiful."

It didn't take her long to learn there was a whole world beyond the shore, farther even than Italy. There were more languages than anyone could count. Some countries were deserts, others were frozen all the time, and some were jungles. It was amazing to her. She wanted to visit every single place, before she realized what a herculean task that would be. She became enamored of maps, reading atlases, and trying to learn as many languages as possible. Every class she took was a step on her eventual journey.

She was seventeen when the man arrived in her sister's bakery. He sat for hours with a single cup of coffee, long enough to attract the owner's attention. When she approached, he asked if she was the Jurick girl who was touting her achievements in college applications. "It's said she speaks three languages."

"Three fluently," Cassiane replied in English. She was working behind the counter. "I am conversant in five," she continued in French.

The man said, "German?"

"Some."

He turned to face her fully. "Would you like to learn more?"

Cassiane, of course, agreed without hesitation. She was gone from Livadeia the following afternoon, her possessions packed away in a cloth bag, tossed in the backseat of the British man's car. She'd gone back home once, for her mother's funeral. It felt like putting on an old shoe, one that was worn-out and no longer molded to the shape of her foot. By that time she had already completed her training and gone on field missions. She had killed and put people in the position to be killed. She'd gone to bed with men and women, both by choice and for missions. The streets of Livadeia were still familiar, but she could no longer see herself in them.

Despite that, she still enjoyed hearing news from her sisters. Rosealine now had four children, only one girl. Her husband was the manager of a movie theater, which meant she'd seen more movies than Cassiane had even heard of. Caterina's bakery burnt down, forcing her to relocate to a smaller shop. It was a blessing in disguise as the lower rent and higher foot traffic meant her profits rose. Every week, schedules permitting, the two families would get together for a Saturday dinner.

By all accounts, it was a perfectly lovely way to live. Cassiane had no interest in it, however. When she read their letters, she dreaded the idea of attending one of the dinners. Tedious small talk. Loud children. It was the world she'd inherited, but she had chosen and earned a place in a world her sisters would find alien and terrifying.

They would never understand this morning, would probably find it thrilling and perilous. Cassiane found it mundane and dull. She woke before the sun rose to meet Constance at the café. They climbed into the younger woman's beat-up Trabi and she drove them to the building where they believed Rudin to be staying. Constance backed the car into an alley, the bumper kissing a dumpster, and unpacked her camera.

"If he truly is a gifted scientist, he will be smart enough to stay behind closed doors until it's time to meet his contact." It was the first thing she'd said all morning, and her voice cracked slightly.Constance either didn't notice the waver in Cassiane's voice or opted to ignore it. "You're probably correct. But everyone has to eat. And human beings tend to rebel against enclosures." She tilted her head in the direction of the Wall and ruminated silently before she continued. "He'll show himself. It may not be wise, or in his training, but given enough time he will come outside. You should know that better than anybody. Considering where you've spent the past few weeks."

"True," Cassiane muttered.

They were speaking German. There was little to no chance they would be overheard, but it was best for the mission if they maintained the cover even when they believed they were alone.

Cassiane had bought breakfast for the both of them when she arrived at the café, and now she opened the bag to retrieve a milk roll. She tore it open, smeared jam inside, and took a bite. Constance passed on eating, instead focusing on the camera which sat in her lap like a docile pet. They were too deep in the alley for the side windows to offer much of a view so they faced forward and sat in silence. The car smelled of freshly-baked dough, which made Cassiane think about her sister. Greece was one time zone ahead, which meant Caterina would already have been up for hours to prepare for the morning rush. She wondered if Cat or Ros ever wondered about her mornings. They thought she was a secretary.

People had appeared on the street. Constance watched them without appearing to examine their faces, chin down and eyes up. There was a light rain falling and Cassiane noticed most of the people passing had hats pulled low, collars flipped up, heads down and faces hidden.

"Will you be able to recognize~"

"Yes."

Cassiane looked at her. "You're positive?"

"I couldn't bring his picture into East Germany, but I studied it the entire journey. I saw film of him. I know his gait, I know how he carries himself, and the shape of his body. I would recognize him from behind, sitting on a bus."

"I'll take your word for it, then."

Constance reached into the bag, retrieved her milk roll, and bit into it.

"Butter? Jam?"

"I like it plain."

Cassiane nodded and faced forward again.

"Did you think you were going to die?"

"When I was shot?" Cassiane shrugged. "Of course. It would have been much easier for Timo to let me die. Safer, too. Either my cover would hold up and I would be burned to ash, or it wouldn't, and the same thing would happen under the name 'Erika Mustermann' like all the other various unknowns who wash up dead on the edges of society."

Constance hummed. "Why did she take the risk?"

Because I think she's in love with me, Cassiane thought. It was something she suspected when they began sleeping together, and her fears only grew stronger each time they went to bed. Occasionally she would wake to find Timo staring at her, or felt her touch on a shoulder, a hip, sliding across her stomach. Her first instinct was to end their trysts and retreat back to a safe, professional relationship. She was surprised by her reluctance to follow through with that very logical plan.

Out loud, she simply said, "You would have to ask her that question."

Constance hummed again.

Cassiane watched the people. A man with a severe widow's peak came out of Rudin's building, not dressed for the weather, and angrily smoked a cigarette. Eventually he was joined by a woman wrapped in a housecoat. Her hair wasn't done. They exchanged words and the woman eventually threw her hands up and stormed back inside. The man continued to smoke for a moment, then walked away down the street. He looked absolutely miserable and half-drowned when he disappeared out of view.

"Not Rudin?"

"No," Constance said.

"I wonder what he did to make her so angry."

Constance shook her head. "He's the angry one. He removed himself before he could say something cruel or strike her. And now he's walking in the rain to calm his nerves. She was trying to convince him to come back inside. If she was the angry one, that would be the start of an apology."

Cassiane considered that. "Maybe she started out angry, which made him angry."

"Possible, I guess."

Silence spread through the car again. Cassiane listened to the patter of rain on the car roof. Constance seemed antsy, like she was the sort who needed to pass the time by talking but was unsure how a continued conversation would be received.

"Do you do that often? Come up with stories about the people you're watching?"

"I'm good at it. Not that it's difficult. People are generally predictable. Couples fight. People are secretly in love with their friends. They resent their coworkers or their bosses."

Cassiane said, "How depressing."

"I find it comforting. Our problems can seem overwhelming until we realize everyone is going through the same thing. Everyone has their own battles. Plus it's fun to make up stories about strangers. You don't do the same thing?"

"It makes them too human. Too real."

"And that's a bad thing?"

Cassiane said, "Enough questions. Timo is supposed to be the psychiatrist, not you."

Constance withdrew and faced forward again.

The street was buzzing with activity now. A man reading a newspaper on his stoop, a woman in work clothes walking her dog. City life. Cassiane let her eyes drift up the side of the building. Several windows had their curtains pushed open so she could see into the apartments at odd angles. She saw the heads of lamps and the tops of armoires. She knew none of these windows looked in on Rudin. He was smart enough to stay hidden, a fact which made her despair that this morning's mission was doomed from the start.

"If he doesn't appear, we can force him to show his face," Cassiane said. "A fire alarm, perhaps. We could pose as two residents searching for a lost pet. Knock on doors."

"We don't want to alarm him. His people probably know how difficult it would be to get a team in place, so he may believe he's in the clear. We can't tip our hands."

Cassiane made a quiet noise of agreement.

"What do I call you?"

"Hmm?"

"Timo calls you Circe. But calling you that seems a bit presumptuous. I'm not a member of your team yet. And I suppose it would be best for our cover if I referred to you as Sophie..."

"Circe is fine."

"Okay. I was excited to work with you. Both of you."

Cassiane looked at her. "You knew who we were?"

"Not before I left Turkey. KYP provided dossiers on you both so I'd know who I would be working with. You both have very high success rates. Reports indicate you've been working well together here in Berlin."

"It's a necessity," Cassiane said. "Either you trust the person watching your back or you die."

"Right."

After a moment, Cassiane decided she had been a bit harsh. "She's a lifeline. The job I do, that we do, it requires cutting yourself off from the entire world. Everyone who sees you is looking through a veil, seeing something false."

"You have your own wall."

Cassiane nodded slowly. "When you're living like that, it's incredibly helpful to have someone who sees beyond it. Someone who knows you."

Constance started to say something, then closed her mouth.

"What?"

"No, it's not my place."

"What?"

"You said Timo is the only one who sees through the wall, but that's not entirely true. She calls you Circe. She uses your code name and not your given name. I know I just agreed to do the same thing but, if it's all the same to you, I'd prefer to call you Cassiane in moments like this. When we're alone and when we don't have to worry about being overheard."

She almost protested, but the idea did appeal to her. And she couldn't exactly tell her that Timo frequently whispered her true name while they made love. On top of that, she actually did like the idea of two people seeing through her walls.

"I suppose that would be fine. What about you? Constance? Is that your real name?"

"Indeed it is. Constance Grimaldi. If you want to shorten it like you do Timo, I'm not averse to being called 'Con'."

"One step at a time, Ms. Grimaldi."

Constance smiled.

Cassiane settled in and crossed her arms over her chest. The odds were against them, but they definitely needed to know what Rudin looked like in order to proceed. They couldn't rely on second- or third-hand accounts.

When the time came, when seconds counted, Cassiane wanted to be absolutely sure who the man was just in case she had to put an end to him.

CHAPTER FIVE

WHILE CASSIANE and Con were on their surveillance mission, Timo closed down the office and walked a circuitous route to a yellow phone box she'd never used before. It was plastered on three sides with flyers, all of which she ignored as she stepped inside and dialed an international number. She was dressed as Dr. Lippert, with a long brown wig and glasses large enough to obscure the shape of her face. Her clothing was also too large so no one could tell if she was big or small. To anyone passing by, she was just another shapeless human form on the street.

The line buzzed in her ear. After a moment, it was answered by a quietly gruff man. "Elegant Pastries."

"Yes, I would like to place an order for seven cupcakes. I'll need them delivered as soon as possible."

"Where can we get in touch with you?" She read the number off the keypad. "We'll be in touch."

Timo kept the receiver to her ear to dissuade anyone else who might come along to use the box. She rested her other hand on the cradle so she could press down the hook switch with her thumb so the line would remain open. Within three minutes, the bells within the phone jangled. She lifted her thumb and connected the call.

"Sunflower," she said.

"Hold please." Silence, then two buzzes. Finally, a new voice, one she recognized and the woman she was trying to get in touch with, said, "I take it your new asset has arrived."

"So it would seem," Timo said. "Initials Charlie-George."

"Confirmed," the other woman said. "She's proven reliable in the past. Talented at gathering information, works well with others, good at building and maintaining covers. We wanted to send an entire team, but we were convinced it wasn't plausible. She's the next best thing. If we could only send one person, I'm comfortable with it being her."

Timo said, "You've worked with her on missions before?"

"Not personally, no. But people I trust have, and they recommend her. That's good enough for me."

Then that was good enough for Timo. "Confirming contact has been made and details of the mission passed along."

"Confirmed." A pause. "The asset is in good shape?"

Timo watched the street through the glass the ensure she wasn't attracting any attention. "She healed nicely after the incident. She dealt with her confinement well, and she's adjusting to her new cover." She didn't mention the evolution of their relationship. Physical and romantic entanglements between field agents and handlers were common knowledge but not openly discussed.

"I'm glad to hear that. Is there anything else to report?"

"No. I'll be in contact if anything changes."

They disconnected the call and Timo stepped out of the box. A brisk wind whipped around the side of the building and slammed into her from the side, strong enough to nearly knock her off balance, but she managed to keep both feet on the sidewalk. She turned to put the wind at her back and walked another indirect route back to Dr. Lippert's office.

She hadn't necessarily doubted Con's identity, but it was nice to have confirmation from those in charge. Now she knew she could trust the newcomer and the mission she'd brought to them. She stuffed her hands deep into her pockets and kept her head down, closing herself off to the other people on the sidewalk who were doing the exact same thing.

\#

"There."

Cassiane was dozing but her eyes opened immediately, focusing through the windshield on the building across the road. Their conversation had dwindled to silence a while ago, and Cassiane saw no reason to remain awake. It wasn't as if she would recognize Rudin even if he made an appearance. Her mentors had told her to never pass up a chance to sleep, snack, shit, or screw, because they could never guarantee when the next opportunity to do those things would present itself. Taking advantage of a nap meant she had to be alert with no warning. That part had taken some practice but she'd eventually learned.

She sat up straighter in her seat. "Where?"

Con gestured with her chin. She already had her camera up at a discreet height, snapping photos. The man stood just outside the building's door, hands in his pockets and shoulders hunched. His shovel-thin face was clean-shaven and his hair looked as if it had been recently cut. He was wearing clothes which were obviously too big for him; the wind pushed the excess material against his chest and around his legs.

"He's changed his appearance, but that's him. I memorized the cliff of his eyebrows and the bridge of his nose."

"The cliff of his eyebrows?"

"How deep his eyes are set in his skull. Whatever this is called." She tapped her own forehead. "It's the one thing you can't change easily or without causing permanent damage. That's him."

Rudin started walking. Cassiane opened the car door.

"Stay here."

She was out of the car and walking before Con had a chance to protest. It wasn't imperative to know where he was going, but leaving the hotel was a big enough risk that it made her curious. If they knew what would make him expose himself like this, it could be used against him in the future.

She fell into step with the rest of the pedestrians, only a handful of downtrodden people reading newspapers or watching their own feet as they walked. Rudin's stride was long and his pace brisk and she feared she might lose him if she didn't speed up. He would be aware of his surroundings and would notice someone rushing to keep him in sight, so she prepared herself for the possibility of failure.

Rudin turned the corner. Cassiane was thirty seconds behind him, close enough to see him jogging across the street while she was still at the intersection. She crossed with the light and, once he was out of sight around a second corner, risked picking up her speed to a fast jog. When she reached the point where she'd lost him she paused and scanned the street.

A barber shop was closest to where she stood. He had no need for that, given how recently he'd changed his appearance. A diner, but she could see that he wasn't at any of the tables or standing in line to order. She didn't think he'd had enough time to reach any of the other businesses, so he must have turned again. She ran full-speed this time and stopped only when she reached the corner. She put her shoulder against the wall and peeked around the crumbling brick.

She spotted him immediately. He was standing by the Metro station, one hand in his coat pocket while he gestured with the other. He was talking to a hunchbacked Vietnamese man, apparently haggling over a price. They finally came to an agreement and Rudin handed over some money in exchange for three small packages. He stuck them into his coat, but Cassiane was close enough to recognize the Lucky Strike logo.

Rudin turned and started back toward her, so Cassiane continued north. She circled the block and returned to where she'd left the car by side streets. There was no need to follow Rudin now that she'd discovered the purpose for his excursion.

She realized the car was empty when she was still half a block away. She slowed down and scanned the street but couldn't see any sign of Con. Instinct told her there was no reason to suspect foul play. It was incredibly unlikely that Rudin had lured her away, purposefully separating them so an unseen partner could abduct the newest arrival to the city. She reached the car and pulled up on the driver's door handle. It opened. She folded herself into the seat and checked her watch. The car was tidy, and Con's camera was nowhere in sight. The other woman would have put up some kind of fight if she'd been taken by force. Cassiane decided her best move was to wait.

Less than five minutes later she spotted Con across the street. The blonde didn't seem to be in any hurry as she waited for traffic and crossed diagonally, head down, arms swinging at her sides. She went to the passenger side and got into the car.

"Bathroom break?"

Con said, "I had my pictures, and I had no idea when you would return, so I thought I would make myself useful. This building really only has three blocks of rooms." She held her hand out. "One is above the lobby, but Rudin didn't come from that direction. The other two are stacked on top of each other, stretching out along the length of the block. I knew that when Rudin came back, he would have to cross that second lobby. So I went into the building and waited."

"Risky."

"Not as much as you might think. The second lobby has a public notice board on the wall and the entrance to the laundry room. When Rudin came back, I was using scrap paper to write a note. I'm looking for a dog-sitter, by the way."

Cassiane almost smiled. "I'll keep that in mind."

"All Rudin saw was a young woman who had just dropped off her laundry."

"No basket," Cassiane pointed out.

"There were four in the laundry room. I just picked one up and let it hang from my fingertips as I wrote the note. Rudin came in and I followed him upstairs. Walked past him as if my room was at the furthest end of the hall."

"What if his room had been the farthest end of the hall?"

"*Scheisse*, my laundry tokens! I am such a fool... Heavy sigh, shake my head, shoulders slump, trudge back downstairs." She nodded at the building. "The fourth window on the second level. The one below the waterspout. That's his room."

Cassiane nodded. "Good work. He may have been suspicious enough to make a note of his neighbors. There's a chance you still managed to spook him just by being an unfamiliar face."

"Maybe. It was a risk I was willing to take. I think he was so terrified of being out in public that he didn't even realize I was there. He practically flew up the stairs." She finally looked at Cassiane. "So? What was so important he would leave his sanctuary?"

"Cigarettes. The stress is probably getting to him. He buys them from a Vietnamese man not far from here."

"Could be useful information."

"Agreed." Cassiane stared at the building a moment longer to burn the location of Rudin's room into her mind's eye. "Any reason to stick around here?"

Con shook her head. "We have the picture and I sincerely doubt he will risk leaving again any time soon. The longer we stay, the more suspicions we arouse. Besides, I want to get these photos developed as soon as possible to make sure I got a good shot of his face."

"Even if you didn't," Cassiane said, "I've seen him now. And odds are good that I'll be the one forced to make a split-second decision about him."

"You're confident you can identify him?"

Cassiane didn't hesitate. "Confident enough to pull the trigger when the time comes. Is that good enough for you?"

"Absolutely."

\#

Timo listened to Cassiane's report of their surveillance, but only perked up when she mentioned the cigarettes. "Did you happen to see the brand?"

"Lucky Strike."

They were in Dr. Lippert's office. Timo had been leaning against the desk, but now she got up and went to the bookshelf. She took down a thick volume and thumbed through it. Cassiane was lying down on the patient's couch, while Con chose to remain standing against the wall next to the door, arms across her chest. She was clearly eager to begin developing her pictures but Cassiane convinced her they needed to brief Timo first.

"This could be very fortunate for us. How long do you think it will take him to smoke all three packets?"

Cassiane shrugged. "He's stressed. He could go through the whole thing in one day."

"That's not good. I was hoping to at least have until the weekend. Con, you're positive you know which room is his?"

"Two thirty-two," Con said.

"What are you planning?" Cassiane asked.

Timo chewed her bottom lip and finished reading the page before she answered. "We can drug his cigarettes. Put something in them to knock him out. I'm not sure what or how yet. Circe, I need you to get a pack of Lucky Strikes. Maybe two or three, just so we have them available."

Cassiane nodded.

"I'll figure out a way to make the swap," Timo said.

"What are we aiming for here?" Con asked. "You said we could put something in the cigarettes to knock him out, but is that the best plan?"

Timo furrowed her brow. "You think we should go full-out? Murder him?"

"It would prevent him from handing over the anthrax."

Timo shook her head. "But we don't know who he's meeting or what they plan to use it for. If Rudin doesn't show up with the spores, they may have a backup plan. We need him alive so we can interrogate him. Find out what his plan is, who his contacts are."

Con said, "Okay, we drug his cigarettes and somehow make

the swap. How do we know when he's smoked the tainted ones?"

"Two birds with one stone." Timo looked at Cassiane and smiled. "Sophie, you're fired."

Cassiane raised an eyebrow.

"Your services are no longer required. Fortunately, it shouldn't be too difficult for you to find gainful employment as a maid at a nearby hotel."

"Housekeeping?" Cassiane said. "Can't I just get shot again?"

Timo put a fist against her eye and faked wiping away tears. Cassiane grimaced at her, which only made Timo chuckle softly.

"It will give you access to his rooms as well as an excuse to check up on him," she explained. "We can't do everything from a car across the street. He's already seen Con in the building, and I'm not a field agent."

"You can clean."

"So you would trust me if I came back and told you I never had an opening to search his room or, if I did, that I hadn't found anything? You'd take my word for it? Or would you wish you'd done it yourself so you could be certain?"

Cassiane didn't respond, ceding the point by looking away.

Timo smirked. "That's what I thought."

Con said, "How do you intend to get her hired? How do you even know if they're hiring?"

"The answer to both questions is the same," Timo said. "There's going to be an open position because we're going to create it."

CHAPTER SIX

THERE WERE two options. One was cheap but morally questionable at best, while the other was a bit more costly. Timo was reluctant to employ the former unless it became absolutely necessary.

Con went back to the hotel in the late afternoon. There was a stone walkway to the courtyard which allowed her to bypass the lobby, and moving with confidence spared her from any curious glances as she proceeded into the main part of the building. Housekeeping was the first room on the ground floor. She knocked and, after getting no answer, twisted the knob and let herself inside. She'd been expecting something as large as a normal room. What she got instead was a glorified closet packed full of cleaning supplies, freshly-laundered linens, towels, toiletries, and anything else the guests might require.

It was the day after her first surveillance mission with Cassiane. She'd gone back to the hotel at sunset and watched three women in matching grey uniforms leave at the same time. They moved like they'd been on their feet for hours and looked forward to finally resting. She took their pictures and went back to her rooms to develop that film, as well as Rudin's picture. The images were now hanging in the secret room underneath Dr. Lippert's office.

Today, she sat outside until the three housekeepers - the same ones from the day before, she was glad to see - had pushed their cart to the far end of the second floor hallway. She assumed that would give her enough time to get in and gather a little information about which woman would make the best target. It was technically possible to follow all three housekeepers home if she recruited Timo and Cassiane, but if there was a chance to streamline their efforts...

The door opened and bumped into her shoulder. The housekeeper leaned in, obviously assuming something had fallen to block the door, and Con took advantage of her distraction to pull the other woman inside. She kicked the door shut with her foot, clapped a hand over her mouth to silence the scream which was already beginning to sound, and pressed her new captive against the wall. She pinned her there with her body and leaned in so their faces were close together.

"I don't need to hurt you," Con whispered. "I don't *want* to hurt you. You've done nothing wrong. Your only sin was that the wrong person chose to stay in the hotel where you happen to work. Just bad luck. It could cost your life, or it could only cost your job."

Tears shimmered in the woman's wide, green eyes. Con glanced down at the name tag pinned to the front of her blouse.

"I want you to walk out of here, Ella. I want you to find another job. I know it will be difficult. I know it may cause hardship for your family. But so would planning a funeral, hm? And if you truly love this job, I believe your position will be available again sooner rather than later. So what do you think, Ella? Can I let you leave this room? Because I would really... really like to let you leave this room."

Ella nodded slowly. Con smiled.

"Good girl."

She released Ella's mouth and took a step back. Ella remained against the wall as if she had become a part of it.

"Go on, then."

"The man who owns," Ella said in halting, accented German. "The..."

Con said, "The owner? Manager?"

Ella nodded. "He likes us. He likes to be touching. Not me. Not yet. The younger ones. He only steals money from me, so far."

"I see."

Ella looked at her again. "So *fuck* this place. But whatever you are doing, be careful." She smoothed her hands over her uniform and gestured at the back wall. "May I get my purse?"

"Of course."

Con stepped aside and put a hand in the small of her back,

gripping the pistol tucked into her belt as she watched the young woman. Ella took a purse off a hook and stooped to retrieve her coat from the floor. She sighed and turned to face Con.

"Are you one of the good guys?"

"*I* think I am."

"That's what they all think," Ella said. "Are you going to hurt people?"

Con didn't know how to answer that, so she chose to be as honest as possible. "We will hurt less people than our opponents plan to hurt."

Ella smiled. "I like that answer. And in that case, I wish you luck."

Con stepped aside to let Ella leave. She stepped over the threshold just enough to confirm she continued off the property and didn't try to warn her coworkers or the handsy boss, then slipped out of the housekeeping room. She used a different route, one which took her to the alley running behind the building so she wouldn't run into Ella. She wasn't entirely certain how she'd stumbled into the best option for getting rid of a housekeeper to create a position for Cassiane, but she wasn't going to tempt fate by examining it.

The important thing was to let Cassiane know before someone else swooped in to take the job and they had to go through the whole thing again.

The rest of the building was so silent that the sound of Timo's shoulders hitting the wall sounded seismic. Cassiane was vaguely aware of the bookshelf's rattle but focused more on pressing as much of her body against Timo as possible. Timo had fistfuls of Cassiane's shirt, holding on near the collar as she allowed herself to be pinned. She spread her legs and Cassiane stepped forward, hips angled forward so Timo could settle against her. Timo opened her mouth in a gasp and Cassiane took advantage with a quick, teasing thrust of her tongue.

The night before, they'd quietly agreed they wouldn't go home together. There was no need to let Con know about their relationship, and it was easier to abstain than sneak around. At least that was what they believed when they made the plan. Cassiane went back to the ghost station room to avoid temptation by sharing a bed with Timo, and spent the night tossing and turning. In the morning she dressed and ascended to the office just as Timo was unlocking the door. They faced each other across the office for a long, silent moment, and then Timo whispered, "Fuck," and flew to her.

And now Timo's hands had relaxed enough to start unbuttoning Cassiane's blouse, while Cassiane was focused more on tugging up Timo's skirt. She moved her hand down and spread her fingers across Timo's thigh, squeezing it to feel the firm muscle through her stockings.

"It was just one damn night," Cassiane muttered before covering Timo's lips again.

"I guess... we... mm... took it for granted." Timo shoved the shirt off Cassiane's shoulders and bent down to kiss and lick her neck. "Tell me how you want me."

She gathered handfuls of the skirt's thick material and pulled until it bunched around Timo's hips. She leaned in, her lips brushing Timo's ear.

"I'm going to get on my knees and put my mouth on you. I'm going to use my lips and my tongue and my fingers to make you scream. Are you wet?"

Timo's eyes were closed. "Uh-huh."

"Give me the words, Timothea."

"I'm wet, Cassiane. For you. Please."

Cassiane brought her hand up to Timo's face, slipping two fingers into her mouth. She watched eagerly as Timo sucked them, each swipe of her tongue making Cassiane's stomach twist. Finally she pulled them free and knelt down to follow through on what she'd just said she would do. The skirt was already out of the way, so she was only delayed by the stockings and underwear. She heard something rip as she pulled the underclothes down around Timo's thighs, but she didn't waste time by investigating. She wet her bottom lip and leaned in.

Timo's body went stiff. Her hands slapped against the wall and she muttered a curse. She didn't understand her own intensity. She'd gone longer than a day without sex, for crying out loud, even in a relationship. But something about Timo was different. Maybe that would fade, maybe they would find a balance or it would fizzle out. Whatever happened, she was going to enjoy it as long as she could.

When Timo got close to orgasm, Cassiane teased her by moving to lick her thigh. Her shirt was now hanging open so she could also kiss and lick around her navel. Timo whimpered at these diversions at first but, once she realized what was happening, responded by grabbing Cassiane's hair and holding on tight. She tried to direct Cassiane, who responded by moving her mouth farther away from where Timo wanted it to be. In spite of how much it hurt when Timo's hand tightened and her hair was pulled. Maybe even a little because of it.

"Oh, god, please," Timo finally grunted, her voice tinged with desperation and anger. "Let me come. Make me come."

Cassiane didn't know how she could refuse, so she let Timo push her head back into position. She used her tongue and fingers to finally push Timo over the edge, savoring each moan and stifled cry as she felt Timo's legs tense on either side of her head. She kept at her attention until Timo pulled her hair again, moving her away this time, and slumped against the wall with a shaky exhale. Cassiane stood and pressed their bodies together, kissing Timo deeply, letting her taste herself.

"Take my clothes off," Timo said as she pushed them away from the wall.

Cassiane obeyed. The blouse fell first, landing on top of the shoes Timo had just stepped out of. By the time Cassiane laid back on the couch, Timo was naked from the waist up. She paused long enough to push her skirt and underclothes off, then focused on removing Cassiane's clothes. Cassiane cupped Timo's cheek, her thumb trembling as she let herself be undressed. When she was naked, Timo climbed onto the couch and put one hand between their bodies, the other braced on the arm of the couch. Their faces were lined up so Timo saw the tightening around Cassiane's eyes as her fingers began to stroke.

"I think you like that," she whispered, her lips close enough that they brushed against Cassiane's mouth.

"I like it very much."

Timo circled Cassiane's mouth with her tongue, then copied the move with her fingertips. Cassiane squirmed underneath her. Her fingers quickly became wet.

"I think you missed me last night..."

"Yeah."

Timo smiled. "Give me the words, Cassiane."

Cassiane grunted. "I missed you last night."

They kissed and Timo built a rhythm with her tongue and fingers. Cassiane lifted her lower body off the cushion to meet each thrust, moaning into Timo's mouth.

The office door opened and Con came into the room. "I don't know if I should knock or wait in the..." She stopped short and then immediately began her retreat. Her hand dropped from the door knob and then began blindly groping for it again to pull it shut behind her. "Jesus, I didn't... I'm..."

Timo was staring at the blonde woman, mouth agape, but Cassiane was too close to worry about being caught. She grabbed Timo's wrist and guided her hand.

"Close the door," she said.

"Right. Yes." Con ducked back into the waiting room. The sound of the door slamming behind her was like an explosion.

Timo put her head down on Cassiane's shoulder. "Fuck, shit."

"Sh. Don't stop. Keep fucking me."

"She could be running to make a report right now."

Cassiane said, "I'll care about that in thirty seconds. Right now..."

Timo bit her bottom lip and stared into Cassiane's eyes, thrusting with her whole body. Her movements were ragged now, angry, and Cassiane pressed the back of her head into the couch cushions in response. Their bodies came together with the sound of slapping, the couch groaning under the strain of their renewed activity. Cassiane spread her legs farther apart, one dropping onto the floor and the other curled around Timo.

"Yes," she moaned. She stared into Timo's eyes, wide and dark and unblinking. "Yes, yes, yes..."

She finally came, stretching out her neck and her fingers sliding across Timo's sweaty skin to pull her closer. They kissed and the tension seeped out of Cassiane, letting her sink into the cushions. Timo dragged her hand up Cassiane's stomach to her throat.

"Now can we discuss this dire situation we've found ourselves in?"

"We don't know how dire it is yet."

Timo looked toward the door. "She could be contacting Control right now. Telling them we're deviants."

Cassiane patted Timo's shoulder to make her get up. She pushed herself off, and Cassiane sat up and retrieved her clothes. She pulled her pants on without bothering to find her underwear first.

"I can tell you exactly what is going through that girl's mind. She's sitting out there thinking about Rudin, and the mission, and the impossibility that Control can get another team into Berlin with the current time table. She's thinking that reporting what she just saw could cause the entire mission to be scrubbed. Rudin will be successful. The Soviets will have their anthrax for whatever their goddamn plot is, and thousands of people will die."

Timo looked at her, hopeful but skeptical.

Cassiane put on her shirt and buttoned it as she crossed the room. "She's smart. She's not going to endanger the mission. But I'll have a conversation with her to ensure she sees things the same way."

#

Con had her back to the door, eyes squeezed shut, one hand over her mouth while she pressed the other between her legs. She hadn't just seen that. She hadn't just walked in on a display of... of... But it was no use lying to herself. She could still hear it through the wall. They hadn't even stopped because they were caught. Her cheeks burned and she pressed the heel of her hand against the crotch of her pants. She was breathing heavily, her voice rising with a series of meager squeaks as she rolled her hips against her hand.

People don't really do that. She repeated the mantra she'd made up when she was a teenager. *That is fantasy, it's made-up, no one actually.. no woman...*

Skin slapped against skin in the other room and Con's squeak became a moan. She was about to flee when she heard voices. Not moans, not sexual grunting, but a conversation. And one of the voices, the deeper one, was coming closer. She pulled her hand away from her crotch and stepped quickly away from the door. She swiped at the tears in her eyes, well aware there was nothing she could do about the burning in her cheeks, and squared her shoulders. She turned to face the door as it swung open and Cassiane stepped outside.

They stared at each other. Cassiane's clothes were haphazardly thrown on. The shirt was untucked and improperly buttoned, and it was clear that she wasn't wearing a bra under it. Her face was red and shone with sweat, her hair mussed and tangled. She was still catching her breath. Con returned her stare, certain she looked like a rabbit facing down a wolf.

"One of the housekeepers walked off the job today," Con said, breaking the staring contest. She looked at the carpet instead, memorizing its pattern of black checks on a field of brown.

Cassiane blinked. "Okay."

"You should get to the hotel as soon as possible to inquire about the position. They may have a waiting list of people who need jobs, so you may only get in if you're actually there in person ready to begin today."

"I understand."

Timo appeared behind Cassiane. She had taken more time to dress and therefore seemed more normal than her partner.

"Good work, Con."

"Thank you." She managed to keep her voice from cracking. "I'll... I should go... get some lunch. And then I'll drive Circe, uh, Cas-Cassiane to the hotel for the job."

Timo nodded.

Con turned and fled the room, eager to remove herself from the situation now that it had been defused. She had no idea how she was going to look either of them in the eye for the rest of the mission, but the important thing was the immediate danger was over. They could focus on the important things. Everything else would, and should, remain on the periphery.

CHAPTER SEVEN

CON HAD calmed herself by the time she returned with sandwiches, though she seemed relieved to see her companions were both dressed. There was a moment of silence where all three of them seemed to be waiting for one of the others to bring up what had happened, but none of them spoke up. Finally Con just held up the bag as a peace offering.

"I got one tuna, one chicken, one ham and cheese. We can fight over them. I have no preference."

They sat around Timo's desk to eat, and she opened her bag to take out three Lucky Strike cigarette packs. She stood them in a row in the center of her desktop.

"I spent last night making these. I was going to explain this morning before I was... distracted."

Con looked away, but Cassiane grinned. She had nothing to hide, and even less to be ashamed of. She found Con's bashfulness amusing. Timo held up one of the packages.

"I got these from a street vendor last night, took them to my apartment, and mixed the tobacco with some powdered methaqualone."

"What?" Cassiane said.

"Quaaludes," Con said. "Where did you get that?"

Timo shrugged. "I'm playing a psychiatrist. My cover requires me to be prepared."

Con raised an eyebrow but said nothing.

"Circe will take these with her into work. When she has an opportunity, she'll swap out the packets in Rudin's room. They take effect quickly and last a few hours, so we won't have to know the moment he's succumbed. I added enough to each cigarette that he'll be in a pliable state. The beauty of this is that it solves the problem of how we'll get him out of the hotel. He won't be fully unconscious, but he'll be in a near-comatose state. We can just tell him to come with us and he'll follow wherever we take him."

Cassiane picked up one of the packets and examined it. She couldn't tell it had even been opened.

"We don't know how he opens the packs. If he cuts them open, if he tears the package... you'll have to do your best to mimic the way it looks."

"I'll do my best."

"That's good enough. Most people don't notice things like how their cigarette packet is torn, but Rudin is on high alert. Anything could be enough to set him off, so don't be sloppy."

Con said, "Did you drug every cigarette in all three packs? That must have taken all night."

Timo shrugged. "I couldn't sleep. I wanted to keep my hands busy." She looked pointedly at Cassiane, then at the couch.

Cassiane couldn't help but snicker. Con blushed, but actually smiled a little.

"Keep that packet. The rest will be backup in case that one gets lost or damaged. Three strikes and we're out. I don't have any more methaqualone and can't it shipped in."

"I'll be careful." Cassiane stood and slipped the cigarettes into her back pocket. She looked at Con. "You said you would give me a ride."

"I did." She wrapped up the rest of her sandwich. "I'll wait outside the hotel in case they don't ask you to start immediately." To Timo, she said, "Then I'll come back here and we can brainstorm ways to get Rudin out of the building."

Timo said, "I'll be waiting. Good luck."

Cassiane led the way out of the office, with Con lagging behind.

The car was parked in the alley. Cassiane waited until they were on the road before she spoke.

"We probably shouldn't be seen together. We don't want anyone to associate the two of us when you already have a connection to 'Dr. Lippert.' It would be too easy for anyone to connect the dots."

"Right." Con flexed her fingers on the steering wheel.

Cassiane watched the road, but in her periphery she could see the tension in Con's body. Her arms were rigid, her posture uncomfortably straight.

"Is there anything you want to ask me?"

Con looked at her, then looked ahead. "Yes, actually. I've been a field agent. I've assumed roles and false identities, like everyone else. But you were deep cover. You were Marta for three years. Saying goodbye to her must have been traumatic. I assume it must have been like losing an actual part of yourself. How did you cope with that?"

"Being shot in the chest helped."

"Right."

Cassiane took pity on the girl. "Marta was real to me. When I was her, Cassiane Jurick was a dream I made up. I was a good and loyal secretary. The mission was always there, but my first mission was getting to work on time, paying my bills, being a good citizen. That's the key to a good cover. Never letting the mask slip, even for a moment, even when the doors and windows are closed and locked. Timo's office was the only place I lowered my guard and let Marta go."

"I suppose I understand."

"I wasn't being flippant. Being shot really did help. I nearly died. I was in agony, delirious, separated from the rest of the world. It was easy to let her go and slip back into my true skin."

"I'm sure having Timothea there helped."

Cassiane nodded.

"The two of you..."

"Will it be an issue?" Cassiane interrupted.

Con swallowed hard. Finally, she shook her head. "No. You don't have to be concerned about word getting back to Control. I've read that intimate relationships in situations like this one are impossible to avoid and may actually help guide it to success. Trust and, ah, bonding. Typically they... There isn't often... um..."

Cassiane rolled her eyes and looked out the window again.

"I never knew anyone actually did things like that. Women."

"Poor thing," Cassiane said. "Timo and I aren't used to having someone who could barge in on us. We were neglectful. We'll try to be more considerate in the future."

"Thank you." Con pulled into the alley across from the hotel again. "Good luck getting the job, Miss Jurick."

Cassiane nodded and got out of the car. She resisted the urge to look back as she crossed the street and just assumed Con was watching her. The fact she and Timo could get caught had always been at the back of her mind, but it was tainted by the very real consequences that would come with such a discovery. Now it was the same risk but without the possibility of imprisonment, reassignment, or death. She wouldn't admit it to Con or even Timo, but having the office door open while they were fucking had almost been enough to push her over the edge to orgasm. Thinking back on it now made her skin tingle as she went into the hotel's lobby.

She would keep her promise to Con. Even if she was feeling mischievous, Timo would preach discretion. But she couldn't help but think being caught again wouldn't be the worst thing in the world. She pushed the thought out of her mind and approached the front desk. A dour-looking man with grey skin rolled his eyes upward to look at her without actually moving his head.

"Hello," she said in German, lips shaking as she put on a hopeful but nervous smile. Timo and Con were now the furthest things from her mind. She could see her grey kitchen, the crackers in the cupboard, the jar on her nightstand with its dwindling contents of paper money and coins. Her fingers trembled as she remembered taking cab fare from it that morning. "M-my name is Sophie. Uh, Rasch, Sophie Rasch." She tucked her hair behind her ears. "I-I was hopeful, hoping, I was hoping you m-might be hiring. I would be willing to take any job."

The man sighed and leaned back in her chair. "This might be your lucky day."

Cassiane let her smile widen, relief flooding her eyes.

\#

Con sat in the car and stared at the hotel. She wished she had a cigarette, though she had a personal rule against smoking on missions. She felt this would be an opportune moment to break that rule.

When she first discovered sex as a teenager, she assumed the other participant could be either gender. It just made sense to her, and she couldn't imagine just being restricted to one option. Her brother overheard her talking about potential boyfriends and girlfriends and sat her down that evening to explain the way things were. He told her that people only got married to people of a different gender.

"But why?"

"That's just the way things are."

"It's a stupid way for things to be," she said. "I don't want to ignore girls. Girls are beautiful."

He had just smiled, called her young, told her things would make more sense when she was older. She saw magazines where women were posing together and kissing, but she decided that was just something they did to sell the magazines. And boys were fine. She got plenty of interest from them, so she might not even have had time for girlfriends. The thought was always there, and sometimes she fantasized about it when she touched herself, but to walk into a room and see it in front of her...

And there was something about Timo and Cassiane. The way they moved, spoke, carried themselves. Cassiane was strong and quiet, but still feminine. Timo had softer features but definitely came off as the more masculine of their team. Was she the man? Was that how it worked? She was the one on top, after all...

Con realized her cheeks were burning but, more importantly, that she had stopped watching the hotel. She pushed thoughts of kissing, of naked flesh, of the smell that had lingered in the office during their lunch, and focused on the building. It was a good sign that Cassiane was still gone. If she'd been turned away she would have come back to the car. That made her hopeful that things were going well.

She kept her mind busy by brainstorming about the next step. They needed Rudin out of the hotel in order for Cassiane to make the swap. They couldn't wait until he went for more cigarettes, for obvious reasons, and it seemed unlikely he would risk another trip for anything less than an emergency. The fire alarm was the easiest option but they didn't know if the hotel even had a working system. If they did, pulling it would bring the fire brigade and far too much unwanted attention.

Ideally, it would be something that didn't break his routine. But that was impossible given the circumstances. His routine was to stay out of sight and wait for some unknown signal. So it had to be something he thought of as his own idea. He had to think he made the decision to leave the room without any external influence. She brushed her thumb over her bottom lip as she thought.

Her mind's eye saw Cassiane's hand resting on the curve of Timo's hip.

"Damn it, stop," she muttered. She squeezed her eyes shut and pinched the bridge of her nose until the image faded.

She looked at the hotel again. The curtains on a ground-floor window had been thrown open and she could see someone in a housekeeping smock moving around inside. She focused on the hazy shape until it got close enough to the glass for her to make out Cassiane's features.

"Well done, Circe," she whispered, drumming her fingers against the steering wheel in victory.

Con left the alley and drove back to Dr. Lippert's building. It was risky for her to be seen there so much, but this was an important day for the mission. Timo needed the information about Cassiane's success. They could brainstorm together about how to get Rudin out of his room. She parked a block away and walked the rest, still plotting in her mind.

Timo was behind the desk and looked up as Con came in. "After this morning, you're still not knocking?"

"Shit... sorry..."

Timo smirked. "I'm only teasing." She tilted her head to look at the empty waiting room behind Con. "I assume, since you're alone, that your mission was successful?"

"I saw Ca-- Circe in the hotel wearing a maid's uniform. She's in place." She closed the door and went to sit on the couch. She paused, remembering what had happened on those cushions, and saw in Timo's wingback chair instead. "So now all we have to do is think of a way to remove Rudin from his room long enough for her to plant the cigarettes."

"Sounds deceptively simple, but it would have to be a pretty compelling reason. Fire alarm?"

Con shook her head. "I thought of that. It's not ideal, but we could go that route if we can't think of anything better. We could get lucky and an opportunity might present itself naturally. Human nature. Most people can't stand being enclosed in a box for long periods of time without getting some fresh air."

Timo said, "Circe just went through the same thing while she was recovering. She was clawing at the walls to get out."

"Is there any way we could recreate that in his hotel room?"

"Not with a window. Do you know if the rooms have central air? We could turn up the heat, make it stifling."

Con shook her head. "I don't know. But even if we could affect his room directly, he would be able to make the adjustment himself when he began to feel uncomfortable. We wouldn't need him to be gone very long. Cassiane could run in and replace the cigarette pack in, what, two or three minutes at the most. Is she good enough for that?"

"Oh, yes," Timo said. "I doubt she would need any longer than that."

"Okay. So we don't need him to make another trek across the city. Maybe we just need him to go to the front desk for something. Noisy people in the next room? He goes to make a complaint?"

Timo thought about that. "He'd be more likely to ignore it. Wouldn't want to draw attention to himself. Or if he did make a complaint, he could call the front desk, or just knock on the door and personally ask them to keep it down."

"Damn it."

Con stared at a spot on the carpet and let her mind go blank. There had to be something they were missing. A simple solution just waiting to leap out and smack them, so obvious, so... She narrowed her eyes and let her focus drift back to Timo.

"We could just... *ask* him to leave the room."

Timo raised an eyebrow. "Doesn't that seem a little conspicuous?"

"Rudin is going to be wary of anything that happens in the next hours and days. He'll be jumpy and anxious. No matter what we do, there's the chance he'll see it as a trick. So we walk right up to his room, knock on his door, and ask him to please come with us. We'll come up with a story about who we are and why we need him. It doesn't have to be particularly clever, it just has to get him out of the room. The fact we're women may actually help sell the fact we're not dangerous. He won't see us as a threat, we're just a pair of weak ladies who need his help with some nonsense."

Timo considered it. "I don't like the idea of playing weak. But it is lovely when your enemy underestimates your power."

"Mm-hmm."

"Okay. We'll work on the straightforward option." She rested her elbows on the desk and leaned forward. "Now that we have the skeleton of that plan, is there anything you'd like to discuss about what happened here this morning?"

Con almost heard an echo of the moans. She managed to shake her head. "I'm not sure what you're talking about."

Timo examined Con's face. She apparently liked what she found, because she nodded and let the tension disappear from her posture.

"Okay. Good." She placed her hands flat on the desk. "Now let's figure out what two helpless young Berliners might need from the strapping gentleman in Room 232."

CHAPTER EIGHT

THE MAID Con threatened had quit immediately. The hotel manager, Ernst, was eager to fill the vacancy as quickly as possible. Cassiane assumed his reasoning involved the other housekeepers, who would have had to work overtime to pick up the slack. After she filled out the barest minimum of paperwork, he escorted her to what she assumed was the same little room Con had found. She was given a uniform that was too tight on top but the skirt was fine. He told her she could wear her own shoes and told her to "find someone to follow, get to work."

She spent the afternoon following Heloise, one of the other maids, who taught her the basics of the job. Vacuuming rooms, replacing the old linens with new, taking out the trash. She figured out the routine by the second room and ignored Heloise's attempts at conversation. Room 232, Rudin's, had a gray BITTE NICHT STÖREN sign hanging from the knob so they bypassed it and went to the room next door.

The room would be a mirror image of Rudin's, so Cassiane took careful note of the layout. The position of the bathroom, the bureau, the safe tucked away on the top shelf of the closet. She thought about how they might use the room. Timo could book it, move in, and then they'd be able to eavesdrop on Rudin. It was a dangerous plan, but it might work under the right circumstances.

Heloise urged her on to the next room. "Don't dawdle. There is a lot of work and many rooms, but only so many hours in the day."

Even though she hadn't started until after lunch, she was exhausted by the time she was finally told she could clock out. Heloise gave her a clean uniform to take home. "Ernst likes to make the tops too tight. This one will fit you better," she promised. "You did good work today. Do it again tomorrow."

Cassiane had to admit she was touched by the praise and the kindness. She thanked the older woman, who left the room with a dismissive shrug and no further comment. Cassiane respected that. Professional but not rude. It was a good combination.

She walked to the office on Regenstrasse. It was after hours so the legitimate businesses in the building had closed long ago. The overhead lights in the lobby were dimmed, and her footsteps seemed to echo twice as much as they did during the day. She felt as if she was entering a mausoleum.

Timo was at her desk when Cassiane came into the office. She glanced up, then let her eyes drift over the unflattering grey uniform. She didn't smile, but her amusement was obvious in the way her eyebrows rose and her head tilted to one side.

"Don't make fun of me."

"Absolutely not." Timo leaned back in her chair. "I was just realizing I hadn't fully thought through the possibilities of the housekeeping uniform."

Cassiane looked down at herself. "Possibilities?"

"For the, ah, bedroom..." She looked away, suddenly bashful.

Cassiane realized what she meant. "Well. I am very good at putting on new identities, if there are games you wish to play."

Timo smiled. "I'll keep that in mind. Con went back to her room so she could get some rest. We came up with a plan to get Rudin out of his room tomorrow."

Cassiane settled into the wingback chair. "I'm all ears."

"I am a poor backpacker from London." Her voice had become meek with the shift to English. She folded her hands in front of her, shoulders hunched, and kept looking from left to right as if she expected an attack to come at any moment. "My car has broken down outside the hotel. I am terrified to be in East Berlin, I barely speak any German, and I am looking for someone who can help me. Please, sir, please, I need help. No one else speaks English. Please, can you help?"

"What makes you think he'll take pity? Or that he'll even open the door to you?"

Timo shrugged. "Con seems sure that he will. She says he'll be suspicious, but he won't be able to leave a woman stranded if it's within his ability to help. I have to take her word for it since she's spent so much time investigating him."

"Con?" Cassiane said.

"Hm?"

"You called her Con."

Timo said, "Oh. We spent most of the day together. She told me to call her that. I think it fits her better."

Cassiane smirked. "You do like to give people nicknames."

"Don't tease," Timo said, chuckling. "We can make it work around your schedule."

"No, move when you're ready. Make sure I know it's happening and I'll find an excuse to get away for a few minutes. Just keep him out of the room for two minutes."

"Will that be enough time?"

Cassiane glared at her.

"Okay. Okay. Just covering our bases. Two minutes."

Cassiane stretched her arms over her head. "I am exhausted. Shall I bunk up downstairs, or..." It was her turn to tilt her head at Timo. "Shall I walk you home, Dr. Lippert?"

Timo said, "Do you think you can restrain yourself under the same roof as me, Miss Rasch?"

"Does that matter anymore?" Cassiane asked. "Constance... Con... knows about us."

"She's not the one I'm worried about. We've already been caught once. We're only fortunate it was her and not someone who could have destroyed our lives. I don't like tempting fate twice."

Cassiane's humor soured. "So are we done? I thought you were eager to meet Sophie Rasch, weary hotel housekeeper."

"I must admit, she is quite appealing." Timo picked up a pen and twisted it between her fingers. "I don't know if we're done. I don't... want us to be done. I just want to maybe take a few days. By that point, we may know Rudin's contact and the mission could be over. It's best to play it safe."

"Fine." She stood and went to move the file cabinet. "I think I will sleep downstairs. I'm too exhausted to walk all the way to your apartment anyway."

Timo sighed. "Circe. Cassiane..."

Cassiane ignored her and descended into the darkness to the ghost station, eager to put as much distance between herself and the rest of the world as possible.

In the dark of the ghost station, with only the distant rumble of passing trains for company, Cassiane stared at the dark emptiness above her bed and thought about what Con had asked her. For three years, she had been Marta. When she went to the market, people who looked at her saw Marta. She was a normal Berliner, with nothing to hide. She worked for a boring man in a boring office and was having a mundane affair with him.

Marta was dead now. No one mourned, no one even recognized the empty space she once occupied. She'd left behind other cover identities before, but she'd never had one ripped away so violently. It was usually when the mission was over and she was moving on to the next assignment. One file closes, a new opens, and she finds out who she will be for the next one.

This time she'd been forced into playing Sophie Rasch while still shedding the skin of Marta. It was like being stuck in an ill-fitting suit with her shoes on the wrong feet.

She knew exactly who she was outside of her covers. She was Cassiane Jurick. She had an apartment in Athens. It was a simple place to rest and relax between assignments. She was rarely there but that was fine. She had a job to do, and that job required her to be out in the world wearing her masks.

She slipped a hand under the collar of her blouse and touched the bullet wound. It wasn't completely healed, but the scar was forming. She ran her finger around its perimeter like it was a crater on the face of the moon. She thought about the nights in bed with Timo, who had covered the scar with her hand or kissed the tender skin just above the wound. The memories made her heart race, and a part of her hated it. Emotional responses meant entanglements.

She didn't want that.

And yet, she hated being alone in this bed. She wanted to roll over and press against Timo's back. She wanted to wake up with the weight of a head on her shoulder.

"Fuck," she muttered, and yanked the pillow out from under her head so she would have something to throw. It impacted the wall with a hollow, unsatisfying thump.

She closed her eyes and let her hands rest on her torso, one on her chest and the other on her stomach, and was eventually lulled to sleep by the intermittent growl of underground trains.

\#

Timo spent the evening in her office. She turned off the lights and stretched out on the couch, watching the file cabinet in the hopes a Cassiane-shaped shadow would rise from it and come to her. She was aware she was the one who caused the argument, and it made more sense for her to go downstairs and make amends if that was what she wanted. But their relationship was dangerous and transitory. There was every likelihood they would be assigned to different agents when this mission ended. It was foolish to expect anything long-term to develop between them.

Still, she hated these nights. Now that she knew what it was like to have Cassiane in her bed, sleeping alone was unbearable. But at some point she slept, and light slowly washed through the window. Cassiane appeared in her work uniform. Cassiane gave her an appreciative once-over before disappearing out into the waiting room. Timo didn't know what Cassiane had found to admire; her mannishly short black hair was tousled from tossing and turning on the couch all night, and she was wearing her undershirt and trousers. She looked a mess.

"I have time to get breakfast from the diner at the end of the street," Cassiane called from the front room. "Would you like something?"

"Coffee. Thank you, Cassiane."

The only reply was the shutting of the outer door. Timo went into the private bathroom connected to her office to brush her teeth. She didn't have a spare outfit, so she would have to go home to find something appropriate for her character. Something cheap and well-worn would help sell the identity of a backpacker. Someone who frequented hostels and slept in train stations more often than proper beds. She heard the door open again.

"Was the diner too busy?" she asked as she came out.

Con stood in the doorway, coat hanging from one hand in the act of hanging it on the rack. She stared at Timo, then quickly looked away.

"Damn it, I forgot to knock again."

"It's all right." Timo retrieved her shirt from where she had left it the night before. "At least I'm partially clothed this time."

"I suppose that's fortunate." Con remained with her face

toward the wall. "Did you mention the diner? I assume Cassiane..."

"She should be back soon. I'm sure she'll get something for you as well." She tucked her shirt into her trousers. "You can look now."

Con relaxed and finished hanging her coat. "Sorry again for just barging in. I'll try to do better about it in the future. Did you tell Cassiane about the plan?"

"Yes. She'll be ready when the time comes to make her move. We have to buy her two minutes. If I can't keep him by the car that long, you have to be ready to intercept him before he gets back inside the hotel. The housekeeping uniform will give her a plausible reason to be in his room if she's caught, but we don't want to make him more suspicious than we need to. A stranger in his room might be enough to make him throw everything out, cigarettes included."

"I'll be ready," Con said. "Once the cigarettes are in place, we just wait?"

Timo nodded. "We'll wait three hours after the switch has been made. That will be long enough for him to crave a cigarette and for the drug to take effect. We'll bring him back here and secure him downstairs. It might not be easy maneuvering a full-grown man, but the drug will make him compliant. It would be nearly impossible if he was completely unconscious."

Con said, "Not to mention harder to explain if we're seen."

"Right. Cassiane did bring up one point of contention. She's concerned about your guarantee that Rudin will open the door to us at all. If we can't get that far, this whole thing falls apart."

Con said, "It's a valid concern, but one we don't need to waste energy on. Our people have been watching Rudin for weeks. He's a considerate person." Timo raised an eyebrow and Con chuckled. "I know, odd trait for someone carrying the means to kill thousands of people, but it's true. He holds the door open for others. He cleaned the gutters for his neighbor. If someone knocks on his door seeking help, even under these circumstances, I believe he will have no choice but to answer the call."

Timo considered the argument and finally nodded.

"Very well," she said. "When Cassiane gets back with breakfast, we'll work out the best time to put our plan into action."

Con smiled. "Let's go get our man."

Chapter Nine

At half past two, Timo entered the hotel through a maintenance door which Cassiane had left open. Their Trabant was parked on a narrow street on the north side of the hotel. She was dressed in shabby traveling clothes: torn jeans, a hooded sweatshirt over two shirts, a knit cap, and glasses thicker than normal to obscure her eyes and the shape of her face. She had a backpack on to lend credence to her cover story and also to change her posture. Being hunched over would make her look like anything but a threat.

She stopped in front of Room 232 and held her breath for thirty seconds. She let it out, then huffed out three times before knocking. She stepped back and grabbed the straps of her backpack with both hands. Her face was red and she was panting when she heard the lock being turned. The door opened a crack, still secured by the chain. She saw a sliver of Rudin's face, just his bloodshot eye and one long expanse of gray skin leading down to the corner of his mouth.

Timo leaned forward and widened her eyes. "Hello? Guten Tag? English, please? Any, any English? I don't have much German."

"I speak English," he muttered.

She smiled. "Oh thank God! Thank you! I've been trying to find, to ask..." She swept her arm helplessly down the empty hall. "No one speaks English, or they pretend they don't..."

Rudin shook his head. "I am sorry, I cannot help."

"No, please!" She held up her hands. "Please, sir. My car broke down outside. I don't have money for a tow truck or a mechanic. I just need to get a few more miles. If you can take a look at it, please, I'm desperate. I can't be stranded here, sir. I don't know what else to do."

He stared long and hard at her. Timo put on her most desperate expression. She let her eyes fill with moisture, her bottom lip trembling. After a few seconds she shifted it to a look of despair, as if she'd decided he wasn't going to help after all. Her shoulders slumped. She looked away. She shrank in on herself and started to turn away.

"I'm sorry I disturbed you, sir." Her voice was meek and hollow. "I-I will find some other way."

She only took two steps before Rudin said, "Wait."

The door closed and she heard the chain sliding. She kept up the façade but her inner voice became very calm as she turned and watched their target step out inside the hallway. He wore a V-neck undershirt tucked into trousers. He glared at her and she could almost see the checkmarks in his mind as he assessed her threat level.

"It is fine." Her voice wavered with tears on the verge of falling. "I don't want to disturb you."

"No," Rudin said. "I will help. But you will walk ahead of me."

Timo feigned confusion. "Yes, of course. I will show you where my car is."

She brushed past him and walked down the hall. She knew he had some kind of weapon on him, though she hadn't seen it. A knife, a gun, something to bolster his courage as he ventured out into the dangerous world. She glanced back to make sure he was following her and gave him a relieved smile. He didn't return it.

"My name is Michelle."

"Mm-hmm."

She faced forward and continued out the door. The metal stairs leading down to the alley echoed under her feet, and she looked back again when she didn't hear him behind her. He was standing in the doorway and examining the street carefully. *Smart*, Timo thought. He was checking for suspicious pedestrians, traps, snipers, enemy agents. It was exactly what she would have done in his place, and it was the reason she had made sure to leave the car in an open area. No dumpsters for an enemy agent to hide behind, no other vehicles parked nearby with someone in the backseat waiting to spring out to grab him.

"Is everything okay?" she asked.

Rudin nodded and finally proceeded down the stairs.

"It stopped just right here. I pushed it off the main road myself, thankfully, but I am uncertain what I would have done if I hadn't found help. Thank you again."

"Mm-hmm," he said again.

Timo popped the hood and stepped back. Rudin stood a few feet away and examined the car, then twisted at the waist to look down the street. There was a man walking his dog at the far end of the block but he had his back to them.

"Sir?" He snapped his head around to look at her again. She held her hands up again. "I'm sorry. You're obviously tense about something. I-is there anything I can do to make you more comfortable? I'm a woman traveling alone in a foreign country, so... so I know the importance of being wary. I don't want to make you feel threatened."

Rudin said, "Will you sit on the curb across the street?"

"Yes, of course." She pointed to a spot where a tree was providing shade. "Will that be okay?"

He nodded and she crossed the street. She sat down and folded her legs in front of her. Once she was settled, Rudin bent down to look into the engine. The Trabant was a very simple car with a very simple engine. She had no doubt he would be able to quickly determine her problem was caused by the fan belt Con disabled a few minutes earlier.

Timo was amused by the situation. She was lying to the man, she was a threat to him, and yet she was able to present herself as a completely innocent stranger. There was no trap, no trick to capture him. Her subterfuge was technically low-stakes but carried the same thrill as any other mission. It was like a game or a trick, mischievous without putting her life at risk. She reminded herself that Cassiane was putting her life at risk and kept track of how much time had passed by counting in her head.

"Your fan belt has come loose," Rudin said.

"That sounds like an easy fix," she said with hope in her voice. *Ninety seconds.*

Rudin reached into the engine and adjusted something. Timo looked toward the hotel and saw Con in the alley, waiting to intercept Rudin on his way back inside. She was holding a German phrase book in front of her and walking at a normal pace which would cause her to cross the sidewalk at just the right moment. If Timo gave the signal, Con would drop the book and spill her bag at Rudin's feet. If their intelligence was right, he wouldn't be able to stop himself from helping.

One-oh-nine. One-ten. Ten seconds left in Cassiane's window, but Timo wanted to give her as much of a cushion as possible.

"That should fix the problem," Rudin said.

"Oh thank you so much. Let me try it..." She crossed the street and got behind the wheel. As promised, the engine grunted to life as soon as she turned the key. "You've done it! You are my hero!"

Rudin put down the hood and waved dismissively as he stepped away from the car. *One-thirty-two.* Technically the two minutes were up, but she wanted to be certain. Con walked past the car without even slowing her pace; there was no need for her to create a distraction. Timo grabbed a ten mark banknote and held it up as she got out of the car.

"Please!"

"No, I cannot take your money." He was already making his way back toward the building. His head was up and he was checking every possible position for coconspirators.

Timo hurried after him. "You saved me so much trouble..."

"Save your money. You will need it. Please, I wish to be left alone."

They were closing in on three minutes. She had to hope it was enough. She couldn't delay him any longer without making him suspicious.

"Thank you! Thank you, sir."

He ignored her and went back up the stairs. Timo watched him disappear through the access door and then went back to the still-running sedan. Con had circled back around and was sitting in the passenger seat. Timo got behind the wheel and drove around the corner where they would be out of sight from Rudin's window and parked along the curb. She checked her watch and then glanced up at the hotel as if she could see through walls.

"Just under three minutes," she reported. "Cassiane said that would be enough time."

Con nodded. "I'm confident."

"Me too."

If all had gone according to plan, Cassiane would let them know by delivering a bag of trash to the dumpster at the opposite end of the alley. That bag would contain Rudin's actual cigarettes. If they were in the bag, that meant Rudin would be smoking a tainted cigarette any moment. He would most likely be under the influence by the time Cassiane ended her shift, at which point they would take him to the ghost station, which they'd spent that morning preparing for his arrival.

Timo checked her watch and waited.

Cassiane saw the Trabi sedan pass by in front of the hotel from the window of the room she was cleaning. She'd planned a lie to get away from Heloise, but when she arrived to work that morning, the older woman told her she could work alone. "You did very good work yesterday. Keep it up. I'll check at the end of the day." It was most likely just an excuse to get out of doing work herself, but Cassiane didn't care. It gave her the freedom she needed to move through the hotel without explaining herself.

She left the room she was cleaning and walked down the hall at a casual pace. She stopped at the head of the stairs. Timo's voice echoed off the cheap plaster walls, but it was impossible to make out what she was saying. Rudin muttered a response, a low growl. Cassiane risked a peek around the corner and saw Timo leading Rudin toward the exit. She envisioned a clock in her head and pushed away from the wall, moving as quickly as she dared without actually running.

Her skeleton key unlocked the door and she stepped inside. The room smelled rotten, the fetor of an enclosed space that hadn't been cleaned in days. Ghosts of countless cigarettes also clung to the walls and every fabric. The sheets and blanket were in a hopeless tangle on the bed. Her housekeeper persona was already strong enough that she was dismayed at the thought of how long would have to be spent getting this room habitable again.

No time. Less than ninety seconds. She saw a cigarette pack sitting on the nightstand next to an ashtray full of smashed butts. She took out her own pack and carefully recreated the rips and tears from Rudin's. She squeezed the sides, bent back the top, and held them up side-by-side to make sure they were close enough to pass muster.

Forty-five seconds.

She put Rudin's pack in her apron and removed all but three tainted cigarettes from the replacement. She put it down on the nightstand, angled it just right, and quickly dashed back to the door. The countdown was still running in her mind. She had gone a little past two minutes. She pulled the door shut behind her until she heard the click, put two fingers against the side of the Do Not Disturb sign to stop it swinging. She stepped away from the door and walked back down the hall like a person who had to be somewhere but was in no particular hurry.

She was almost to the stairs when a man called out to her. "Miss."

Cassiane stopped and slowly turned. Rudin was standing in front of his room, his broad shoulders blocking the light from the open door at the opposite end of the corridor.

"Towels," he said. "I would like... I need towels... please."

"Of course, sir. Room number?"

He gestured. "Two three two."

Cassiane nodded. "I'll get some to you right away, sir."

"Sorry. Thank you." He was muttering so she could barely hear him, his head lowered as he fumbled with his key to unlock the door.

She was already out of sight by the time the door closed behind him. She went to where she had left her cart and grabbed a trash bag off its side. She stuffed the stolen pack and the leftover tainted cigarettes inside, cinched it closed, and twisted it a few times before tying two knots.

Downstairs, across the courtyard, into the alley. She saw the Trabant at the other end of the alley with the shadowy silhouettes of Con and Timo visible through the windshield. She didn't acknowledge them. She simply lifted the top of the dumpster, tossed the bag inside, and brushed her hands together as she pivoted to go back inside.

There was something she hadn't registered when she was in the room, but could now acknowledge its importance: there were no smoldering cigarettes anywhere. Not propped up in the ashtray, not carelessly left on the nightstand or the table. The only butts she saw had already been snuffed. Being summoned outside by a stranger and being so close to running out of cigarettes would make him stressed. Rudin would almost certainly light one up immediately upon returning to the room. He might be smoking a tainted cigarette at that very moment.

Their countdown clock had begun.

CHAPTER TEN

CON VOLUNTEERED to retrieve the trash bag, since Timo and Cassiane had already put themselves in danger during the mission. She pushed a box over so she could stand on it and lifted the lid. She spotted it immediately: a white trash bag tied closed with two knots. She snatched it up and hurried back to where Timo was waiting. Her hands trembled as she plucked at the first knot with her fingernails.

"You can just rip the plastic," Timo suggested.

"Right. Yes."

She grabbed with both hands and pulled until it tore. Inside she could see loose cigarettes scattered like kindling, as well as a battered pack with three cigarettes still inside. She smiled and held up the packet so Timo could see it.

"She did it."

Timo smiled and held out her hand. Con clapped it in her own and pulled Timo to her for a hug. The front seat of the car was like a couch, so there was no central console to awkwardly navigate for the hug and Timo scooted closer so she wouldn't be leaning. Con was very aware of the move, even more aware of Timo's hands on her and the feel of their cheeks touching. When Timo pulled back, Con turned her head to place an impulsive kiss on Timo's cheek. She accidentally caught the corner of Timo's mouth.

"I'm sorr–"

Timo turned her head just enough to make it a proper kiss.

Con cupped the back of Timo's head, taking advantage of a mistake caused by adrenaline and excitement at a mission well-done. She thought Timo was beautiful, and after what she'd seen the day before, the thought of actually giving in to her instincts had never been far from her mind. And now she was kissing a woman, trying to enjoy the experience but also distracted by analyzing the moment. Was it better than kissing a man? It certainly wasn't worse, and a part of her mind was running through a film reel of all the women she could have kissed in the past but never did.

When she sensed they had gone on too, long, Con moved her lips back to Timo's cheek and grabbed a handful of Timo's hair to pull them apart.

"I'm sorry," she gasped. Her eyes were closed and she was suddenly furious at herself. "God. Cassiane is never going to forgive me."

"Don't," Timo said. "Cassiane... We're... I don't know what is happening there. Maybe nothing anymore. But don't... d-don't worry about her. It was the adrenaline of actually succeeding with this plan, sticking our hand in the lion's mouth only to come out unscathed. The excitement got the better of me." She touched Con's cheek. "You're a beautiful woman, Con, and I cannot bear the thought of a beautiful woman who regrets kissing me. So please say you don't regret it."

Con smiled. "No regret. No regret."

Timo leaned in and Con very softly said, "Yes," just before their lips met. It was a softer and more deliberate kiss this time. Timo took the lead, her hand warm where it lay on Con's chest, on top of the highest button of Con's blouse. Her mind immediately went to the button being undone, to Timo's hands on her skin, sliding lower to places which had only been groped by rough but well-meaning men. Timo would know what she was doing, she would know how to...

"Stop!" Con said, shoving Timo back.

"I'm sorry," Timo said.

Con faced forward. She shielded her eyes with one hand as she struggled to compose herself. She was trembling.

"Don't be sorry," Con said. "Never be sorry. I... I just needed it to stop while I was still thinking clearly. We're... We shouldn't still be sitting here."

"You're right." Timo started the car but hesitated before she put it in gear. "We have a few hours before the end of Cassiane's shift. We could go back to the office to wait."

Con didn't look at her.

"We wouldn't have to do anything," Timo said. "But we also wouldn't have to stop."

Con swallowed hard. "That sounds like a good way to pass the time."

Timo nodded and backed out of the alley.

Con explained her inner turmoil on the drive back to the office, explaining her confused early attraction toward women and subsequent shame when she was told it was wrong. Timo recognized elements of her own history in the tale.

Timo remembered being a young woman in Heraklion, trapped by the borders of the island. She could still see the tall stone fortresses in the harbor which made her feel as if she was in a prison. She only had her father, a man who was so relieved by her tomboy nature that he didn't bother to examine what it meant. She called herself Tim or Timmy, she hung out with boys, she cut her hair short. It wasn't necessarily that she wanted to *be* a boy. But she saw girls, lithe and olive-skinned and smiling girls, and she saw how they fawned over the boys at school, and she wanted those girls to see her in the same way.

She kissed her best friend's sister. She was punched by her best friend for it. The taste of lip gloss mingled with blood. She kissed her best friend's sister again a few days later, without the blood. She didn't know what she would've done if she grew up thinking that kissing girls was impossible. The wonderful evenings she would have missed out on...

Timo also took the time to consider whether or not she was betraying Cassiane. They hadn't made any sort of commitment to each other. Based solely on their conversation the night before, whatever they'd shared might have come to an end. She didn't feel she owed anything to Cassiane, or that the kiss and whatever came next was being unfaithful. Above anything else, she believed that in the same situation, Cassiane wouldn't be debating the morality of her choices.

When she parked, she reached over and put her hand on top of Con's. "Was that your first kiss with a woman?"

Con kept her eyes forward but slowly, she nodded.

"Thank you for letting me be your first." Con leaned in again, but Timo put her fingers against the blonde's lips. "Inside."

"Right. Of course."

They left the car and went into the building. Someone on an upper floor was shouting, his voice echoing down the stairs, but they ignored it as they went down the dark corridor to Dr. Lippert's office. She reached for the light switch but Con stopped her.

"No. Please."

Timo let her hand linger near the wall, the door ajar so the hallway light fell past her onto Con's face. "Nothing has to happen right now. We can just make sure everything is in place for the end of Cassiane's shift."

"I want it to happen. But I think if the lights are on, it'll make it harder for me to let it happen."

"Okay."

She left the light off and closed the door. She stepped forward and collided with Con, who was already moving toward her. Timo took a step back and allowed herself to be pressed against the door, her hands on Con's back, letting the other woman take the lead. She parted her lips as an invitation and felt the uncertain flicking of Con's tongue.

"Like this," she whispered, and demonstrated with her own tongue.

Con made a soft mewing sound and angled her hips against Timo's.

"I'm not a virgin," Con whispered.

"Okay."

"I've been with men. I... I don't want you to think I'm some innocent..."

"Shh." She brushed her lips across Con's again. "That's an important part of it. Don't talk about doing it. Just let it happen."

Con grabbed Timo's hair with both hands. Timo allowed herself to be guided toward the couch, even as part of her questioned the ethics of being with someone else on the same couch where she and Cassiane had so recently had sex. She didn't have time to debate that question as she fell onto the cushions and let Con land on top of her.

"Am I too heavy?"

"You're fine... I like it..." She slid her hand down Con's side. "That kind of talking is okay. Telling me what you want. What you don't want. What you like. That's very good talking."

Con nodded. Even in the darkness, Timo could tell her eyes were closed. Her breath washed across Timo's face in unrhythmic waves. Timo moved her hand to the front of Con's slacks.

"I like that," Con whispered.

Timo lifted her head and pressed her lips against Con's throat. She worked her fingers through the folds of Con's tucked-in shirt, pulling it free until she felt bare skin. She poked her tongue out in concentration and inadvertently licked Con's neck.

"I-I like that," Con said in a near-gasp.

"Do you?" Timo moved her mouth up to Con's ear. "How much?"

"A lot."

Con had settled her full weight on Timo, shoulders hunched, hands still on the back of Timo's head. She was pushing against the other arm of the couch with both feet and her entire body was taut. She whimpered and gasped as Timo managed to stretch out two fingers and stroke the crotch of Con's underwear. Her forefinger smoothed out the cotton and her middle finger pressed against it before moving in slow circles.

Con pulled Timo's hair. "I like that, Timo."

"I like it when you say my name," Timo said.

"I like the way it sounds." She gasped and hunched her shoulders. "Oh, shit."

Timo whispered, "It's okay."

Con shuddered and lifted her head, stretching her neck out. The couch frame groaned as she pressed her feet against it and Timo worried it might collapse, but Con went limp first and settled her full weight on Timo.

"Is this okay?"

"It's great." Timo crossed her arms behind Con, her hands flat on the blonde's back. She smiled when she realized they were both fully-clothed. "Are *you* okay?"

Con didn't answer immediately. Her shoulders rose and fell with her breathing.

"Con? Are you asleep?"

"No. I don't know how to answer that question. What we just did... I feel like I just stepped of a cliff. And I'll keep walking as long as I don't look down. I don't want to look down, but I also don't know how long I can keep my head up."

Timo moved her hand into Con's hair. "Then close your eyes and let me carry you."

"God," Con whispered, and pressed her face against Timo's throat.

Timo stroked Con's hair. They needed to make sure everything was ready for the night, when they would have an enemy agent in the ghost station. But knowing he would be there was reason enough to value this last opportunity to have a quiet moment together. So she closed her eyes and listened to Con's breathing.

Cassiane struggled to focus on her work. She knew they wouldn't make a move until the end of her shift, but she couldn't help wondering if Rudin had started smoking yet, if the drug had taken effect, if he was just lying in his room waiting to be swept up. She had to be patient. Moving early could ruin their entire plan. So she cleaned rooms. She made beds. She emptied the trash and stuffed damp towels into her cart. She was glad for the hypnotic nature of cleaning messes in rooms which were all but identical to each other.

She had just stepped out of Room 250 when she heard a door close further down the hall. She looked up at the sound and forced herself not to react when she saw Rudin had stepped into the hallway. He stared down at his room key as if he'd forgotten what it was, then slipped it into his jacket pocket. He took a step, seemed to misjudge the length of his stride, and swayed wide to the left. His shoulder struck the wall and he let out a heavy 'whumpf' before pushing himself upright again.

"Shit..." Cassiane looked to make sure they were alone in the hall before she approached him. "Sir? Is everything all right?"

He shook his head like a child. "I didn't ask for anything... what?" He looked at her, looked behind himself, and then started walking again. "It's fine. Okay."

Cassiane put a hand on his elbow. "Sir..."

Rudin spun on her, grabbed her throat with one hand and her shoulder with the other. "You do not touch me! I am leaving here!"

His breath reeked of tobacco, a thick cloud so strong that it seemed as if the air had turned a blackened yellow. She couldn't risk another housekeeper or even a guest seeing this encounter. She brought both hands up into the V formed by his arms and swept out against both of his elbows. His grip weakened when his arms bent, and she jabbed the flat edge of her left hand against his throat. Rudin gagged and fell backward, clutching at his neck.

Cassiane grabbed the lapels of his coat and hauled him back toward his room. He made a feeble attempt to escape, kicking his heels against the carpet and slapping at her arms, but the drugs and their initial grappling had taken the strength from him.

When she was in front of Room 232, she retrieved the key from his pocket and unlocked the door. She grabbed him by the coat and dragged him into the room. She stepped out into the hall to make sure he hadn't dropped anything and saw Heloise standing at the end of the hall staring back at her.

Cassiane straightened and squared her shoulders. The older woman's expression was unreadable.

"In twenty-four hours," Cassiane said just loudly enough to be heard, "your life could be exactly the way it was before you set eyes on me. Or, in twenty-four seconds, it could be over. You are not my enemy."

Silence stretched out until Heloise finally said, "You were not a terrible housekeeper."

"I had a good teacher."

Heloise sniffed, either dismissing the praise or a subtle laugh. She shook her head and pivoted on her heel, walking back to the stairs.

Cassiane went into Rudin's room and kicked the door shut behind her. Rudin seemed to have fallen asleep on the floor. She hooked her hands under his arms and hauled him across the room to the chair. Her legs and back already ached from the work she'd done that day, but she managed to get him up into the seat. Rudin moaned and slumped over as soon as she had him positioned. She forced him upright and slapped his cheek.

"Mr. Rudin. Look at me."

"I am so tired. I was going to buy cigarettes. I'm out of cigarettes..."

That would explain his stupor. She'd left the drugged pack only an hour earlier. She knew nothing about the drug, but she feared taking that much in such a short amount of time could cause an overdose. Their original plan had been to get him into the ghost station and then come back to search his room for the drug he was supposed to deliver, but she didn't want to let this opportunity go to waste.

"Where is the anthrax, Mr. Rudin? Can you tell me that?"

He opened his eyes and stared at her, brows knit in confusion. "No... no, you can't..." He looked toward the bed and lunged for the nightstand.

Cassiane brought her knee up. He collided with it, blood spurting from his nose as he fell back into the chair. Cassiane went to the drawer he'd been reaching for and pulled it open to discover a small black doctor's bag.

"Who are you?" Rudin murmured, eyes closed again.

Cassiane took the bag and walked to the door. "Just housekeeping, Mr. Rudin. You get some rest, and I'll see you again very soon."

She tucked the bag under her arm, turned off the lights, and left Rudin alone in the dark.

CHAPTER ELEVEN

THE GHOST station had been transformed from Cassiane's sick room to a prison cell. Timo and Con moved the bed and other furniture into the basement, leaving only one chair in the center of the space. Timo brought down her tools to bolt the chair's legs to the floor while Con attached straps to the arms and back. Timo could sense Con felt awkward about what they'd done, so they worked in silence so she could process it.

"Was what we did wrong?"

Timo looked up from where she was kneeling. "Depends on who you ask, I suppose. I know our superiors would be very upset about it, which is why we're not going to tell them. I could give two shits what they think, however." She tugged on the leg of the chair to confirm it was secure before moving to the next one. "Or do you mean from Cassiane's point of view?"

"I was speaking generally, but I suppose I would like to know what she would think."

"Cassiane isn't the type of person who gets jealous. And I cannot imagine she would ever get jealous about me, or what we have. Had. Whatever. I would be very surprised if she has strong feelings about what we did in either direction."

"Good. I suppose that's good." She finished attaching the last arm strap. "Do you believe this will hold him?"

"It's held larger men," Timo said. "If he's being particularly destructive, we can drug him again. I have some more potent things upstairs which will keep him calm and pliable."

Con checked her watch. "Cassiane's shift is nearly over. We should head out."

Timo nodded her agreement. They left the overhead light on so they wouldn't be fumbling in the dark when they returned with a stumbling and drugged Soviet agent.

Cassiane saw the Trabant parked across the street and grabbed the doctor's bag before running out to them. Timo rolled down the driver's side window and Cassiane passed the bag through.

"What's this?"

"It has the item Rudin was planning to hand over. I got it from his room."

Timo arched an eyebrow. "Explain that."

"He smoked all three cigarettes that were left in the pack. He was in a stupor and tried to go buy more. We got into a scuffle in the corridor and I had to drag him back into his room. The alternative was letting him get hit by a car or arrested by the local police. I figured it was the best option and it saved me the trouble of coming back tonight to look for the item."

"Risky, but smart," Timo said. "Is he still in the room now?"

Cassiane said, "I haven't heard a peep from him since I left him. I also, ah... My superior saw me dragging Rudin into his room. She's been avoiding me all day, but it seems my cover is blown. We don't have to wait until the exact end of my shift to make our move if you're ready."

Timo looked at Con, who shrugged and nodded.

They got out of the car and followed Cassiane back into the hotel. Timo brought up the rear since she was the only one who hadn't been inside yet. When they got to the second floor, Cassiane gestured for Con to wait at the head of the stairs. "If he tries to run," she said. Con nodded and tried to look inconspicuous. The hallway was just wide enough for Cassiane and Timo to walk shoulder-to-shoulder. Timo cleared her throat and spoke in a quiet voice.

"Circe, there's been a development you should know about."

"After," Cassiane said.

Timo began to argue, but seemed to accept that as the wisest course of action.

Cassiane unlocked Room 232 and stepped inside. Rudin had moved to the bed, sprawled facedown on top of the blankets. His shoulders jumped when he heard the door open but he couldn't summon the strength to lift his head and see who had come inside. Timo went to the far side of the bed near his feet, while Cassiane moved close to his head.

"Mr. Rudin?" Cassiane spoke heavily-accented Russian. "We're going to take you somewhere now. What do you think about that? Would you like to go for a nice car ride?"

"I have to stay here..." His voice was muffled due to his lips being pressed against the blanket. He still hadn't opened his eyes. "You're not supposed to be in here. You must go. *Bitte nicht stören.*"

Cassiane looked across the bed at Timo. "You're certain he will be able to walk under his own power?"

"We just have to get him on his feet." She leaned across the mattress and slapped his arm, also speaking Russian when she addressed him. "Mr. Rudin! We're going to take you to get some food. What do you think about that? A nice hot meal? A big bowl of solyanka soup or varenyky. How does that sound?"

"Solyanka?" He finally lifted his head. "I have been starved..."

"We know, Pavel, we know. That is why we're here. We just want to take care of you. Stand up and my friend and I will get you all you can eat."

Rudin put his hands flat on the bed and tried to push himself up. Cassiane helped him get upright, and Timo positioned herself under his right arm. Cassiane moved under the left and put her arm across his waist. Rudin rested his weight on their shoulders but was standing on his own. They escorted him to the door and into the hallway. She looked toward the stairs and Con motioned them forward, indicating the path was clear.

Rudin's head was lolling as if his neck had become rubber. "Rot Front."

Cassiane and Timo exchanged a look. "What does that mean, Mr. Rudin?" Timo asked.

"I would also like very much some Rot Front... with my varenyky..."

Timo nodded that she understood. "Candy. Yes, Mr. Rudin, we will have some for you when we get to where we're going. Just keep walking, okay?"

His body tensed and he lifted his head. "Wait! My bag. I need my bag..."

"The black bag from your nightstand," Cassiane said. "We have it, it's in the car, it's safe."

"Are you positive?"

Cassiane patted his chest. "Yes, it's all taken care of, Pavel. Just keep walking." They had reached Con, so Cassiane nodded down the stairs. "Make sure the way is clear."

Rudin muttered, "I don't think I should go anywhere."

"Just come with us, sir," Timo said. "Everything will be perfectly fine."

The stairs were a trial, and both women suffered aching arms to prevent Rudin from tumbling down headfirst. He was muttering under his breath about food when they left the hotel. Night had fallen outside while they were in the building, as if a sheet had been drawn over the city. Con had opened the driver's door and pushed the front seat down. Cassiane put a hand on top of Rudin's head and ushered him into the car, letting him collapse on the bench. She shoved him aside as gently as possible and then climbed in beside him.

Timo said, "All settled?"

"I think we'll be fine."

Rudin was slumped against the far side of the back seat, chin on chest, hands folded in his lap. Timo was confident that Cassiane would be able to control him during the short ride back to the office, so she pushed the front seat back up and got behind the wheel. Con still had the black doctor's bag and held it in her lap when she got into the passenger seat.

None of them wanted to jinx the mission with congratulations, so all three women were silent as Timo put the car in gear and pulled away from the curb.

Rudin had fallen asleep by the time they got to the office. Cassiane had to wake him, and then all three had to haul him from the backseat. He was a large man made larger by the fact he wasn't particularly interested in helping them. It was worse than moving dead weight, because a dead person wouldn't randomly change direction or pull left when they needed him to go right. Con went ahead with the doctor's bag to make sure the lobby was clear. She stood at the foot of the stairs to listen, then waved Cassiane and Timo through.

"Is this where the food is?" Rudin slurred.

"Yes, it's downstairs. It's a very secret kitchen, so you have to be quiet. Can you do that, Mr. Rudin?"

"Mm-hmm. Very silent."

"Good man."

Con was their advance guard. She opened the office door, moved the file cabinet, and ensured nothing got underfoot as they marched Rudin to his eventual prison. He lifted his head once they were in the basement. His eyes were closed, but he had a dreamy smile on his face.

"I can smell it... borscht! There's borscht!"

Cassiane raised an eyebrow at Timo, who shrugged. She couldn't smell anything.

Con opened the door to the ghost station. Cassiane examined the space as she entered but said nothing about the changes as she guided Rudin to the chair. It was positioned so he would sit facing the door. They turned him around and Timo put a hand on his shoulder to gently urge him down.

"Here we are, Pavel. Have a seat."

He dropped into the chair and exhaled sharply, as if he had been doing the majority of the work for the past few minutes. Timo's arms felt suddenly weightless, as if they would float up without a concerted effort to hold them own. She flexed her fingers until that drifting sensation faded and bent down to secure the straps around Rudin's ankles. Cassiane strapped in his right arm, while Con came into the room to do his left. He looked down at what they were doing, confused.

"Wait... how... I can't..." His eyes widened and he lashed out, flipping his left arm up. He backhanded Con in the face and she fell backward. He reached for Cassiane, grabbed her throat, and squeezed. "Let me go. Let me go this instant or I will~"

Timo, who hadn't yet stood up after securing his feet, was kneeling in front of him. She knew she couldn't physically force him to let go of Cassiane's neck so she took the only option presenting itself to her and punched him in the crotch as hard as she could.

Rudin howled and let go of Cassiane. She recovered quickly and threw herself across his lap and finished tying up his left arm. Con had gotten back on her feet and stood behind the chair, both arms around Rudin's neck to hold him against the chair. Cassiane pulled the straps tightly across his chest as he thrashed and fought, spitting and cursing at them in Russian.

Once every strap had been pulled tight and he was securely held to the wooden frame, Cassiane lifted herself off of him and stepped back.

"Calm down, Mr. Rudin!"

He called her a whore in his native tongue.

She punched him in the face.

"Calm. Down."

Rudin glared at her. "They send girls now? Is that all your people have left? All the men died in wars, cowering in dog shit, and this is what you're reduced to?"

Cassiane said, "I feel like punching him again."

Timo said, "Perhaps it would be best to fight that feeling. Come. Let's go. We should give Mr. Rudin some time to think about his current predicament."

He spit on the ground.

The women walked from the room, but Cassiane paused at the threshold. She looked back at Rudin.

"I spent some time down here recently. It can get very, very lonely."

She reached out and turned off the light, then shut the door behind her and left him alone in the darkness.

Once the door was closed, Timo reached for Con's cheek. "Are you okay?"

"It was just a slap. Cassiane is the one you should be worried about."

Her concern was real. There were bright red marks on Cassiane's throat, which she tried to cover by putting her hand over them. Timo brushed her hand away and examined the skin. Con also deflected Timo's attention because she was ashamed of what happened in the room. Cassiane got hurt because of her. If Rudin had managed to get both hands free, or if he'd been able to squeeze hard enough to cause permanent damage, or if he'd...

"I have to go," she said, brushing past Timo and heading back to the ladder.

"Constance," Timo called after her. She stopped and looked back. "Don't leave the building. From now on, two of us must be here at all times."

Con nodded and climbed up into the office. She put her hands on Timo's desk and hung her head, eyes closed, finally taking a deep breath and holding it. She was shaking and on the verge of tears. She'd never had such a horrible lapse during a mission. She'd also never even come close to such a disaster. It was only logical to assume it happened because of the liberties she'd taken with Timo.

Karma or fate was punishing her.

"Never again," she swore to any deity that was listening. "I will never touch another woman like that again. Let this mission go well, let us return home safely, and I will remain chaste."

A tear fell, shaken free from the thought of finally experiencing something so magnificent only to have it torn away from her. But she had to think of the greater good. She smoothed her hands through her hair and pulled (*just like Timo had pulled it when they were kissing*) and tied it loosely to keep it out of her face.

For the rest of the mission, she would be entirely professional. She wouldn't risk another slap on the wrist from the universe.

Cassiane leaned away from Timo's examination. "I'm fine. You think I haven't been choked before?"

"All the more reason to check for cumulative damage." She glanced toward the ladder to make sure Con was back in the office. "There's something I have to tell you. The thing I almost told you at the hotel. I figure now is as good a time as any. Con and I were intimate this afternoon after we retrieved the cigarettes."

"She's queer?"

Timo said, "She wasn't sure. We confirmed things."

Cassiane arched an eyebrow and smiled. "I bet you did."

Timo laughed nervously. "You aren't upset?"

"Why would I be upset?" She sounded legitimately confused.

"Because we're... you and I were..." She shook her head. "Never mind."

Cassiane put a hand on Timo's arm to keep her from turning away. "Sex is sex. Maybe what you and I were doing will become something. Maybe it won't. Maybe you're supposed to be with that girl up there, maybe you're not. You're not going to figure things out in one afternoon, or fucking me for a few days under bizarre circumstances."

"I was worried you might be jealous."

"I like you very much, Timothea, and I really hope the last time we were together wasn't the actual last time. But you're not my property. I don't decide what you do, or with whom."

Timo touched Cassiane's neck again, gently, and stroked upward toward her ear. "So you still want to do those things with me?"

Cassiane's cheek twitched. She looked toward the closed door to the ghost station. "Of course I do. I enjoy it more with you than with... with most."

Timo smiled and moved her hand to cup Cassiane's cheek. "Are you really okay?"

"I'm fine." She brushed Timo's hand away, not unkindly. "You really ought to be checking on the girl up there. I don't think she's used to that sort of violence."

"I'll check on her in a moment. It will give her a chance to compose herself."

Cassiane nodded and, at that moment, Rudin released an animalistic howl. Cassiane was positive it echoed off the brick walls of the closed station, but it was doubtful that it would be heard in the building above. Maybe commuters on a passing train would hear it, but they would definitely mark it up to the overall creepiness of this forbidden stretch of underground.

"We could simply kill him and be done with it. We have his spores."

Timo shook her head. "Not until we know who its intended recipient was. We have no idea what their plan is. They might have a contingency. This was merely the first step in our mission."

Rudin howled again, but the sound was weaker this time.

"Do you want to go back in?"

"Absolutely not. We'll give him time to expend his energy, and let the drugs wear off. Once he's exhausted and resigned to the fact he's been captured, then I'll go in. And I'll make him tell us what we want to know."

CHAPTER TWELVE

TIMO STEPPED into the ghost station and turned on the lights. Rudin squinted and twisted his head away, flexing his arms against the leather straps. Timo placed the chair she'd brought in a few feet away from Rudin and sat down.

"Could you do me a favor and not scream while I'm in here?" She spoke his native Russian. "It's quite annoying. Shout your head off when it's just you, but I know the ringing in my ears would linger for hours afterward."

"You're British."

"If you like." Her Russian was accented with French now. She crossed one leg over the other and studied him casually.

Rudin returned her stare, then snorted and looked away. "And yet you don't wear a mask."

"What would be the point of that?" She switched to a Spanish accent, just because she could. "You've already seen all of our faces. Masks are itchy."

"What is this place?"

"It's your new home, Mr. Rudin. I'm not sure about the yellow brick, but I think the architecture is quite nice." She eyed the walls and tilted her head. "Is it yellow? Maybe it's burnt ochre…"

He closed his eyes and took a deep breath. "I'm still feeling whatever you gave me. It's difficult to think, to stay awake. I think my adrenaline is pushing me through the cloud for the time being." He was slurring his words. "What was it, anyway?"

Timo said, "Witchcraft."

"I think... the maid. She was in my room while you distracted me with the car. She put something in my water glass, or..." He smiled and rolled his head back. "My cigarettes. You poisoned my poison."

"You came to Berlin for a reason, Mr. Rudin. You brought a very powerful weapon with you. We just want to know what you intended to do with it."

He breathed in through his nose again. It reminded Timo of meditation, as if he was trying to clear his mind through sheer will.

"We all think of the other side as villains. Monsters. You probably justify this - drugging me, holding me hostage - by telling yourself I'm some silent-movie villain eager to tie damsels to train tracks. You people, whoever you might be and wherever you're from, you tell yourself we're evil so you can live with the things you do to us. We do the same thing to you."

Timo said, "Your point?"

"We both have the same goal. Not... not literally, of course, but in general. We've seen suffering and we want things to be better for our people. The other side wants bad things for our people, so we must do awful things to protect them."

"The greater good," Timo said.

He nodded slowly. He still hadn't opened his eyes. "Exactly so."

Timo leaned forward with her elbows on her knees. "How many people were you planning to kill for your version of the greater good? That drug of yours is no half-measure."

"And how many of my people have yours killed? No one leaves the battlefield innocent, ma'am. And this is a war, it always has been. There's always a war, always soldiers. Sometimes we're hidden but we're always fighting."

"Then let's end it," Timo said. "At least this part. You don't have to kill anyone and neither do we. Tell us what we want to know. You admit that we are the same, that I am only a version of you from the other side of an imaginary line. Help me keep my people safe."

Rudin shook his head slowly. "It's defensive."

"A preemptive strike."

He finally looked at her. "You expect us to wait until we are bloodied and weak before we attack? Would you hesitate and allow your enemy to hit you first, to kill dozens of your people, before you raised a hand against them?"

"The hands were raised long ago," Timo said. "And you are correct, wars never end. There are only periods of rest where everyone prepares for the next one. Peace doesn't exist."

To her surprise, his eyes were full of tears. He said, "The world we live in. The world we inherited and seem intent on maintaining. Brutal and cruel."

"Who are you meeting? What do they plan to do with your anthrax?"

"I won't help you. My part in this mission is obviously over, but it can still succeed without me."

Timo lowered her head and bit her bottom lip. It was exactly what they'd feared. Rudin and his anthrax were merely one piece of a larger plot. They'd managed to steal one bullet but their enemies still had a gun hidden somewhere. She stood and lifted her chair, carrying it with her back to the door.

"Wars may not end, Mr. Rudin, but they are full of battles. This is a battle you have lost."

She turned off the lights and stepped out, pulling the door shut behind her.

"You're welcome to scream as much as you like now."

Cassiane waited outside the door, back to the wall, listening to the muffled voices coming from the other side. She looked up as Con came back downstairs but didn't say anything to the girl as she leaned her shoulder against the other side of the door and tilted her head closer to the wall as if that would help her hear better.

"You don't have to worry."

Con looked at her. "What?"

"Timo told me what happened."

"Oh." Her eyes widened and she looked down at her feet. "You aren't angry?"

Cassiane sighed. "If I was acting like a possessive ass, you would both rightfully think I was being unreasonable. So why do I have to defend my lack of anger? It doesn't make sense. Even if I cared, it would be ridiculous to let feelings interfere with a mission like this. We both had sex with Timo. We both enjoyed it...?"

It took Con a moment to realize Cassiane was waiting for confirmation. "Oh. Um, yes, very much so." She blushed.

"And Timo enjoyed it as well. That's the only important thing." She crossed her arms and faced forward. "This is a stressful job. Take your relief where you can get it."

Con made a quiet noise of consideration and then fell silent again.

A moment later, the door opened and Timo emerged from the ghost station again. She shut the door and looked at Cassiane. She put down her chair and realized Con was standing behind her. She motioned for them to follow her away from the door.

"It's what we feared," she said under her breath. "Whoever Rudin was meeting, they have a contingency. Losing the anthrax won't stop whatever they have planned. We have to extract the information from him somehow."

Cassiane nodded and began unbuttoning her uniform blouse. Timo held up a hand to stop her.

"Let's not resort to violence just yet. He seems fairly reasonable. I think, given enough time, we could get him to tell us what we wish to know."

"We may not have time," Con said. "We have no idea when the meeting was going to happen, but it must be soon. If they show up and Rudin isn't there..."

"He'll talk faster if we beat it out of him," Cassiane said. "It sounds as if we don't have time to be squeamish about it."

Timo said, "I'm not being squeamish. If we go to that extreme this quickly, we'll have no way to escalate. On top of that, if we beat the information out of him, we'll have no choice but to kill him when this is all over."

Cassiane raised an eyebrow. "That wasn't the plan to begin with? He can't leave here alive, Timo."

"If we can convince him to help~"

"We will never be able to do that, Timo!" Cassiane hissed. "Let alone in the short time we have. The meeting could be happening right now. Every second we stand here debating the inevitable is one second closer to an attack. To hundreds of deaths on our heads. We've already come this far."

Con's voice was soft, almost soothing. "If our positions were reversed, do you believe he would show us any mercy?"

"If our positions were reversed," Cassiane said, "he would be able to kill one of us so that the others would know he's serious. You know that's true, Timo."

Timo said, "I don't want to compare my actions to what I believe my enemy *might* do in my place. I want to imagine we're better than him. That we stand on the higher ground."

Cassiane shook her head. "Believe that all you wish. In my experience, all higher ground gets you is a better view of the carnage."

Con winced but lifted one shoulder in a meager shrug. "I agree with Cassiane."

Timo paced away from them and then slowly back. She rubbed the lower part of her face, cupping her chin in a caricature of deep thought before she looked at them again.

"Perhaps you're right, but it's my call. I want to try. I saw something in there. I saw a human being, someone whose mind can be changed if we make an effort. At least give me a chance to *try*."

Cassiane walked away without saying anything, tacitly giving up the argument.

Con said, "I very much hope I'm wrong."

"Me too," Timo said.

Con went to join Cassiane by the door and Timo, clearly aware of the lines that had just been drawn, went back up the ladder into her office. They could take first watch while she tried to get some sleep.

It was going to be a very long night.

Timo went back into the ghost station. Rudin didn't blink at the lights this time, and she didn't bring a chair with her. She turned to the left and began pacing the perimeter of the room with her hands clasped behind her back. She imagined the station as it had been before the Wall; newspaper kiosks, shoeshine stands, people rushing about to catch their trains. The far wall would be gone, replaced with a row of men and women dressed for work. The near wall would also be gone, in its place a flight of stairs leading up to the street. The early-morning stench of cologne mingling with perfume, a fug of flowers and cigarette smoke above it all. Now it was so grave-silent that Timo's footsteps echoed.

She didn't speak until she was directly behind his chair. "Your name is Pavel Rudin. No middle name. Your father worked for the allies in World War II. He was already old when you were born. You grew up hearing stories about the work he'd done in the war. You probably thought he was a superhero. Using science to defeat the bad guys. That's why you followed in his footsteps."

Rudin didn't react. She was in front of him again so she could see his face.

"But the world has changed since the days when your father

served his country to protect the world. Alliances shifted. Now the bad guys are the same people Leonid Rudin served with. The people you're working with, Pavel, are they planning to attack the Americans? London? Are they targeting the sons and daughters of people your father may have considered friends?"

Rudin said, "The world evolves. If Father were alive, he would see the necessity~"

"Your father would be a traitor?"

"No, he~"

"That's what you just said, Pavel. You said that your father would turn on his allies. Kill his allies."

"Allies who turned their backs on him first! We were abandoned~"

"You are petty children who are angry because you didn't get your way," Timo said, "and now you lash out at people who should be your friends."

Rudin said, "You call yourself friends? Ridiculous. You hold a gun against our heads~"

"We're holding guns against each other's heads."

"You hold a gun against our heads," Rudin shouted over her, "and treat us like demons when we dare defend ourselves! Stay in line or risk nuclear war! You Americans claim~"

"We're not American."

"Then you are their patsies, saving them from getting their hands dirty. That is the United States' chief export! Sacrificial lambs. You kill me, my people eventually kill you, and the heroic Americans get what they wanted while claiming to be on the side of the angels."

"So your anthrax was going to target a nuclear site? A military base?"

He started to respond but caught himself and quickly looked away. Timo examined his body language carefully. She softened her voice and moved closer to him. She bent down to look into his eyes.

"It's not, is it? You were going to infect civilians. Some great hero... making people sick, killing them, all to make a statement. How many women, how many children. You call yourself freedom fighter, I call you terrorist."

"Two words for the same thing," Rudin muttered. He was looking at the floor now. "We do what we must to further the cause. I do what I must, and you do the same."

"There are lines."

He met her gaze. "And this is not beyond your line? Holding a man hostage, drugging him, threatening him with violence? That is within your comfort zone?"

"No. Not *innocent* men. Only men who intend harm on a massive scale. Only men who see the lives of civilians, strangers, as expendable pawns in a game they don't even realize is being played."

Rudin looked away again.

"Tell me who you're meeting and when. Tell me what they have planned. Do something right, Pavel. Do something that would make Leonid proud."

"Release just one of these straps and I assure you, I would make my father very proud."

Timo straightened and sighed. "I'll give you some more time to become reasonable." She walked to the door and turned off the light. She stood there for a moment in the darkness.

"The woman you choked earlier. She has lines, too. They are different than mine. If you don't cooperate soon, I will move my line, and I allow her to come in here to try her methods."

She opened the door and left him to consider the threat.

CHAPTER THIRTEEN

CON FELT the need to be as far away from Timo and Cassiane as possible, so she took it upon herself to search Rudin's hotel room. She got the key from Cassiane and left the building, opting to walk the relatively short distance rather than taking their only car. It was late enough to be dangerous for someone to be walking the streets alone but she was too distracted to care. Distracted by her failure, by Cassiane's lack of reaction to what happened with Timo, worrying they had succeeded in the first part of their mission only to run out of time for the most important part.

All the streetlights on the hotel's block were out, casting the building in deep shadows which were only broken by light from a handful of windows. It reminded Con of mountains she'd seen in the desert. They were pockmarked with caves where thieves and vagabonds would hide, their fires giving away their location.

The courtyard entrance was blocked by a large metal security gate. There was probably someone on duty in the lobby who would let her in without asking any questions, but she didn't want to announce her presence unless she absolutely had to. She picked the lock, slipped inside, and locked the gate again behind her.

The hallway lights were dimmed, but she could hear TV and music playing in most of the rooms she passed. When she reached 232, she knocked and listened carefully for movement within. There was no reason for management to even know Rudin wasn't coming back or for the room to have been given away to new guests, but she wanted to be positive before she barged in. She had just taken the key from her pocket when the exterior door opened and a heavyset woman stepped inside.

Con stared at the woman, both of them frozen where they stood. She had already threatened one housekeeper and was hoping not to make a habit of it.

"You are... friends with this man?" the woman finally said.

"No."

The housekeeper pressed her lips together. "You are friends with that other woman, then."

Con nodded. "We're just trying to do what's right. We're trying to save lives."

"I assume the other woman won't be coming back for her shift tomorrow."

"No, probably not."

"Good. She was a shit maid."

Con couldn't help but smile. "I'm not sure I'll tell her that. If it helps, she won't come looking for payment for the time she worked. No one would notice if you claimed you could deliver the check and it just... vanished."

"Not like she had much coming anyway..." She shuffled onward, moving to pass behind Con. "You won't be causing a ruckus around here, will you?"

"No, ma'am. We took him away from here so we wouldn't cause you any problems."

"Good."

Con opened the room and tapped the Do Not Disturb sign. "Leave this alone until his checkout time, okay?"

The woman had already passed her. Without turning, she waved dismissively. "One less room for me to clean. No problem."

Con stepped over the threshold and shut the door behind her. She turned on the light and examined the mess. She breathed the scent of the room without judgement, although she had to admit the odor was powerful and disagreeable. Once she felt at home in the space, she unfastened her belt and began undoing the buttons on her shirt.

A moment later, she was completely naked. She gathered her clothes in a pile next to the door, not bothering to fold them, and went to the drawer next to the bed. Rudin had packed lightly, with only a single suitcase. While he hadn't utilized the hotel's housekeeping services, he was forced by necessity to use the laundry room at the far end of the ground floor. She opened the bottom drawer and found two outfits.

The pants were much too large for her, as was the shirt, but a pair of suspenders kept them from falling down, and tucking in the tails of the shirt at least gave the impression of a smooth line. She stood up straighter and squared her shoulders. "Pavel Rudin," she whispered. She lowered her voice and lifted her chin. "Pavel Rudin. Pavel. I am Pavel. Pavel Rudin." She smoothed the shirt over her stomach and paced the floor in front of the bed. She curled her toes in the carpet and closed her eyes. She had a very important appointment. There was something very dangerous in her doctor's bag. She was going to hand it over. Soon.

But when? Where? To whom?

Con opened her eyes and noticed one of the room's chairs had been moved closer to the window. Someone sitting in it could watch the street through the gap. She walked over and took a seat. She sprawled her legs wider than she normally would and slumped lower on the cushion. Rudin hadn't necessarily chosen how he would sit in the ghost station, but she mimicked his posture as best she could. The ashtray was well within reach from this position. She wondered if the drugs Timo had put into them would still be dangerous as ash and made a note to take it with her when she left, just in case.

She was Pavel Rudin. She had come all the way from Dubna for this meeting. Every person passing on the street outside was a potential threat. This room was her only sanctuary. Her palms were clammy so she rubbed them on her pants. She mimed bringing a cigarette to her lips and stared at the wall directly ahead of her.

This was her sanctuary. Her only safe haven in the entire country. She obviously had to kill time. Maybe her contact was coming from farther away. Maybe she couldn't guarantee when she would arrive so they set a date and couldn't risk further communication.

So here she is. Behind enemy lines and far from home waiting for a ticking clock to finish counting down.

She scanned the room and didn't see a clock from her current position. Rudin hadn't been wearing a watch. That implied he was waiting for a day, not a time. The bag had still been in the drawer. If the meeting was imminent, his anxiety would have caused him to move it somewhere more prominent. The dinner table, the armoire, the foot of the bed. Somewhere it would be in his sight and easy to grab. He would want it close by.

He had also been going for more cigarettes when Cassiane subdued him. If he thought his wait was almost over, he would might not have needed to refresh his stash.

Con lifted her head and narrowed her eyes. She realized she didn't know where to buy cigarettes. She'd never been to East Berlin and, according to their intelligence, neither had Rudin. So how did he know where to go?

She stood up and looked at the room through Rudin's eyes. Someone knew about Berlin. Someone had told him about this hotel and where to buy cigarettes. Maybe this person had also set up the meeting. Whoever arranged it would have to be a person Rudin trusted and who knew the city well enough to choose a perfect clandestine rendezvous. There must have been papers. Notes, maps, correspondence, evidence of a plan which had gotten Rudin to this point. He may have memorized everything, but she doubted that.

There was a safe on the top shelf of the closet, but she ignored that. She would obviously check it before leaving, but she had no doubt it was empty. Locks didn't mean security to Rudin. The safe would be an obvious first stop for anyone searching the room, but such a person would already have bypassed the door lock. Putting secrets in a safe would be the same thing as keeping them pinned to the wall with a giant neon arrow pointing at it.

If the locks weren't enough to protect his secrets, then he would use another measure. Time was the easiest security to manufacture. He hid his papers in order to force his enemies to search the room, keeping them occupied long enough that he could come back and catch them in the act. There was one piece of art hanging on the wall, but it looked too heavy and unwieldy for one man to remove by himself. Her gaze drifted lower to the heating vent. Possible, but only slightly better than the safe. Rudin had spent hours in the room with nothing to do but think of places to hide sensitive information. He wouldn't just stick it in a hole or behind a painting.

A black vinyl wall base ran the perimeter of the room. She ran her eyes along it until she had to move to see around the bed. There, next to the nightstand, the vinyl had been pried away from the wall just enough to leave a gap. She doubted there was enough room behind it to hide anything, but it was the tell that she'd been looking for. She walked over and crouched down, pulled the vinyl away from the wall, and hooked her fingers under the edge of the carpet.

The tacks came up easily. She smiled at her own cleverness and pulled it further, revealing several much-folded pieces of paper on the concrete below.

Con spread the papers out on the bed and smoothed down the creases so they would lie flat. It seemed to be one continuous piece of correspondence rather than a series of letters. The top of one page was addressed to "PR." Everything after that was encoded, but she scanned it anyway. Codes were good for concealing a message from being immediately read. What they couldn't do was disguise the shape of a conversation. A two-letter word here, a single letter here. She could already tell the code was crackable, but she didn't have the time. She would work on it back at the psychiatrist's office while Timo questioned Rudin.

The other page was a map of the city. Rudin was too smart to mark anything other than the hotel's location, but it still might be useful to them somehow. She refolded everything and stacked them on the armoire where she could retrieve them on her way out.

She checked the heating vent and behind the artwork but, as she'd suspected, found nothing there. She assumed the code would be something easy, something his stressed mind would have no trouble remembering, and she was correct. 2-3-2-7, the room number with a random number tacked onto the end. Seven was the second number she tried, a very common lucky number. Within the safe she found a handgun with two boxes of ammunition. She took it all, slipping it into the pockets of her trousers.

Someone knocked on the door, but she ignored it. She made sure she had all of the papers. The person outside knocked again. She looked at the clock and knew she would either have to answer or wait for whoever it was to go away before she could leave. She rolled her eyes as the knock came for a third time, this time with an angry but breathless shout.

"Open up! Right now!"

Con opened the door. The manager, whose name Cassiane had told her was Ernst, glared at her. The maid she'd spoken to was cowering in the hall a few feet away.

"I don't know who you are," Ernst said, "but you owe me one hundred marks."

"Incorrect," Con said.

He blinked, then narrowed his eyes. He slapped the door. "One occupant! One! Big Russian man makes one, you are two, extra charge for two."

Con looked past him at the maid. "Are you Heloise? I don't blame you for telling him about me. I assume he runs this place quite strictly. You must have been worried about your job."

Ernst waved a hand in front of her face. "Don't talk to her! We are talking and you owe me one hundred."

Con remembered the maid she'd threatened so Cassiane could take her job. She remembered the warning about the manager, the liberties he took with his staff. She kept her eyes on Heloise.

"This man. He steals from you? Tips, wages. Maybe he does more?"

"Do not speak to her!"

Heloise didn't answer, but her body language confirmed Con's questions.

"Okay," she said.

The gun would be too loud. She didn't know how many other guests were in the hotel, but she couldn't risk it. Plus it would be extremely messy. Too much of a hassle. So she grabbed him by the collar of his shirt and hauled him into the room. She bent her arm at the wrist, feet planted, and slammed him hard against the wall next to the door. She clapped her free hand over his mouth and nose, then shifted the position of her other hand to his throat. His eyes were wild, furious above her hand. She squeezed so he couldn't open his jaw to bite her hand.

She stared into his eyes and saw the fear creep into them, saw the realization that he wasn't dealing with the type of woman he normally victimized. Subordinate women, women who couldn't afford to make a fuss, who had to take whatever he did to them out of fear of something worse. She stared, unblinking, and saw him understand that he had no power over her. He threw his hands at her torso, but he was no fighter. His fists bounced off her ribs leaving nothing but a slight soreness in their wake. It hurt when he kicked her shin, but it only made her squeeze harder.

"Don't kill him," Heloise said from the doorway.

"Sh," Con said.

Heloise looked down the hall, panicked and afraid. Con considered Heloise's plea. She hated this part of herself. The violent part, the part which reminded her of her father. He had been an angry person. Drunk. Cruel. When she recognized those tendencies in herself, she pushed them down along with her questions about her sexuality, hiding it all under a stone in her mind, focusing on her education. That led her to the KYP, to a job where violence was occasionally necessary.

"Better, worse, or the same?" Con asked.

"What?"

She still hadn't broken eye contact with Ernst. His anger was gone now, replaced with fear. "Would your life be better, worse, or the same without him in it?"

Heloise blinked. Her eyes were full of tears and her face was bright red. "I-I don't know. More difficult at first..." She swallowed a lump in her throat and looked at the floor. "But there are other girls who work here. Their lives would be better without this man. But you don't have to kill him."

"I don't have to," Con agreed.

She pulled him away from the wall, kicked his knee, and followed him as he collapsed onto the ground. She put her body on top of his and with a motion as quick as blinking, broke his neck. She heard a sharp inhale behind her and looked back to see Heloise looked green around the gills.

"If you're going to throw up, do it somewhere else."

Heloise fled.

Con looked down at the body underneath her and sighed. She didn't like the idea of what she had to do next, but it had become a necessity.

Over the next ten minutes, she moved Ernst's body onto the bed. She stripped off his clothes and replaced them with the underwear she'd discarded when she came into the room. She loaded one bullet into Rudin's gun, placed the weapon in Ernst's hand, and twisted his arm so that the barrel was resting against his temple. She put his finger around the trigger and pulled. The force of the explosion was enough to make the bed shake, and the hollow pop seemed to echo off every surface in the room at a staggered interval.

The police would be summoned and find a deviant who had finally taken himself out of his misery. It probably wouldn't even warrant a full investigation. Someone might notice the broken neck, but she doubted they would pursue the mystery. People who did odd things during sex were mentally deranged, the police might say, it's a wonder he didn't do it sooner.

Setting up the display made her feel far sicker than the actual murder. The police would think the same thing about her if they knew what she'd done with Timo. Deviancy and shame went hand-in-hand, didn't it, and surely anyone suffering from this affliction was doing the world a favor by removing themselves from it. She wondered if any of the police officers who responded to this call would look at the scene and feel shame for his own secret fetish, and she hated herself for it.

She couldn't worry about that now. Ernst was a difficulty in her path and he needed to be removed. This was the most expedient way of achieving that goal. She squeezed her hands into fists to stop them shaking and checked her clothes for signs of blood. She hadn't intended to wear Rudin's suit home, but she couldn't take the time to change now. Someone in the hotel might have already called the police. She gathered her clothes and the papers she'd recovered and pulled the door shut behind her as she left.

She fully expected she would have to pick the lock on the courtyard gate to get out, but she was surprised to find Heloise waiting there, holding the gate open with one hand.

"I'll need to let the police in," she said, pushing it wider to let Con out.

Con nodded to her and ran off into the night.

Chapter Fourteen

Cassiane took a lamp from Timo's office and placed it in front of the ghost station entrance. She removed the bulb and turned it. When she opened the door, all Rudin saw was a blinding beam of light shining directly at him. He recoiled as if she'd splashed cold water in his lap, twisting and squeezing his eyes shut so hard that his face looked like a fist. Cassiane shut the door but left the overhead lights off. She didn't need them.

She stood in the dark and waited. She could hear his breathing. The rumble of a train in the distance was no more distracting to her than her stomach growling at lunchtime. This was the room where she had died and come back to life. This had been her womb, her whole world. She didn't need lights to know every inch of it, and nothing in it could distract her from the task at hand. She started to pace, her footsteps quiet on the floor tile.

"Which one are you?" Rudin asked.

"The one who had to make promises to get into the room alone with you. Do you want names? You can call me Circe."

Rudin laughed quietly. "The villain appears. Your friend attempted to use logic to gain my cooperation. When she failed, she sent in the monster. To scare me. To threaten me with physical violence."

"No, actually, she was very insistent that I not harm you. We disagreed about that, but she won the argument. For the time being, anyway. I'm just here to get a feel for you as a person. You've been abstract before now. Sitting here, you're a real person. Living and breathing. Real people are different than ideas. Pavel Rudin is different from a Soviet agent. I was curious to know who we're dealing with so I can plan accordingly."

"You can't even see me."

"I've seen enough of you, Mr. Rudin." She reached the false wall, the one separating their ghost station from the tracks. "This is something different. I can see it better in the dark."

He laughed again. "Look all you want, Miss Circe. The other one already tried to get inside my brain and appeal to my humanity. What about your humanity? Don't you care about what your people are doing to mine? The crimes they've committed?"

"Everyone has committed crimes. No one's hands are clean. I don't waste much time thinking globally. I know what's happening here and now. One man, planning to cause an untold number of deaths. That's an easy decision to make."

"The trolley problem," Rudin said. "Pull a lever to sacrifice one person in order to save five."

Cassiane said, "This is not a hypothetical riddle about morality. You stand with a gun to the head of an innocent person, threatening to pull the trigger, and I have the ability to knock the gun from your hand to save them."

"You have a peculiar definition of the word innocent."

"And you have a maddening definition of humanity. You care about others. Hell, we took advantage of that to get into your hotel room. You showed compassion for a stranger. How could someone put himself at risk to help a person in need be the same man who unflinchingly provides the means to kill so many others?"

Rudin was silent. She could hear his breathing.

"Of course," she said. "It wasn't an unflinching choice, was it? You're still not certain about the part you're playing in this scheme."

"It is necessary. Our enemies, *you*, have made it necessary."

Cassiane said, "Preemptive strike, counterstrike, retaliatory strike, repeat. All until someone can't get back up again. You don't have to take part in that, Mr. Rudin. You can end it now. You can step out of the cycle and maybe let it collapse."

Rudin said, "You would pull the weapon from our hands and leave us defenseless for whatever the Americans have waiting for us next."

Cassiane crouched in front of him. The darkness was

complete, with not even a small amount of light to let her eyes adjust, but she had pinpointed his voice. She knew the room well enough to know she was looking directly at him.

"It is not my job to promote reason," she said. "I leave that to the other one. Call her Medea. When she fails, I bring my fists. I bring pain. I break fingers, legs, toes. I pull teeth. It's not an attractive specialty, but it works more often than talking. It's much faster, too. But I know there are times when it isn't going to work. That won't work on you, will it? Pavel. You would let me break every bone in your body before you told me who you were going to meet and where."

He was silent.

"The trolley problem doesn't tell you who the people on the tracks are. If they are good people or bad. Maybe the five people are criminals. Maybe the one person is a man simply doing his job. It doesn't tell you why they're on the tracks or why they can't move. What if the one person is deaf? Does he deserve to die because he can't hear the train coming?"

"What is your point?"

"Morality exists in the moment, Mr. Rudin. No resentment, no fear of future reprisal. I told you I don't think globally. I think very small. I don't know what decisions brought you here with a bag of poisons. You came. You plan to kill a great many people. It is my moral duty to stop that from happening."

She stood up and moved closer so she could lower her voice.

"If my friend is not successful, it will be proof enough to me that you will never see reason. I've already determined torture won't work on you. So at that point, you will be worthless to us. You'll be eliminated. And I assure you, Mr. Rudin, I will make it hurt."

"You just said you know torture won't work on me."

She could hear the tremor of fear in his voice. She reached into her pocket and removed the item she had placed there before coming into the room. It was just a matchstick, the type that could be struck with the bottom of a shoe, a brick wall, a concrete floor.

"The pain won't be a means to an end," she said. "It will be pain for pain's sake. It will be solely to ensure that you suffer before you draw your final breath. If it becomes clear we cannot save the lives you're putting in danger, I will take some solace in making you suffer as well."

"I suspected you would kill me when this is all over. And yet you call yourselves heroes."

Cassiane snorted. "I said no such thing. It doesn't matter what country I call home, the history books are either full of atrocities we committed or beautiful lies that paint us as heroes. Every successful kingdom on the globe is fueled by bloodshed. I'm not a hero, Mr. Rudin. I'm just a person standing at the lever deciding which track I can live with."

She closed her eyes and flicked her thumbnail across the matchstick's flint, igniting it in a flash of bright yellow. Rudin had been staring directly ahead with his eyes wide open and pupils dilated. He recoiled, his brain telling him it was a flash of gunpowder even as his eyes stopped working. She blew out the flame and cast the room back into a darkness that was even more complete for him now.

"Think, Mr. Rudin. Think very hard."

Cassiane straightened and left the room. Timo was waiting for her outside, arms folded over her chest, close enough to the door that she could have eavesdropped on the conversation.

"I didn't hurt him." She looked down at the match, smoke still curling from its tip. "Not much, anyway."

"I heard. Do you think you got through to him?"

Cassiane shrugged. "I don't really care." She started toward the ladder, and Timo followed. "The timeline on this is too tight and he's too dedicated. If we haven't made progress getting him to talk by tomorrow evening, we should kill him and consider the mission a failure."

"We won't know it's a failure until the people he's working with go through with their plan."

"And we have no way of knowing when that is," Cassiane said. "We won't recognize the awful event as one we might have prevented. We could spend the next month working him, and it won't matter. One more day and then we should cut our losses and end the mission."

Timo looked like she wanted to argue, but Cassiane knew she had no tactic. Finally, she dipped her chin and said, "One more day."

Cassiane returned the nod and ascended the ladder to the office.

\#

Con tensed when a shadow in the corner of the office moved, but she relaxed when she realized it was just Cassiane climbing up from the basement. She had been standing with her hands flat on

Timo's desk, head down, trembling. The adrenaline from her adventure had faded, leaving her jumpy and unable to catch her breath. She hadn't even bothered turning on the lights when she got back to the office, hoping she would be able to compose herself before anyone knew she was back.

Cassiane stood on the other side of the desk and stared at her. "Everything okay?"

"Yes." She nodded and stood up straight. "Everything is fine."

"Why are you dressed like that?"

She had almost forgotten she was still wearing Rudin's clothes. She'd dropped the clothes she'd worn to the hotel next to the door in the waiting room.

"It's a long story," Con said.

Timo had also climbed up into the office. "What's wrong?"

"Nothing is wrong." Con held up the papers she'd retrieved from Rudin's room. "I got these out of the hotel room. A coded letter and a map. Nothing very useful on the face of it, but if we can crack the letter, it may lead us to something important."

"Why are you dressed like a man?" Timo moved closer and touched the lapel of the jacket. "Whose clothes are these?"

Con averted her gaze, inadvertently letting it fall on Cassiane. "They're Rudin's. I put them on when I got to the hotel. I do it often when I have to search someone's private space. I put on someone's clothes to see things through their eyes. To get into their head. Usually I change back into my own clothes before I leave, but there were issues with that this time."

"What kind of issues?" Timo said.

"I had to kill someone. The hotel manager."

Cassiane put a hand to her forehead and turned around. Timo pressed her lips tightly together and closed her eyes. Con explained everything that happened in the hotel room as concisely as possible.

"I won't claim it was the right decision, but it was the choice I made in the moment. It was going to be an issue either way, whether I let him live or not. He may have blackmailed us. He may have turned us in for his own benefit. He is the sort of man who is less problematic as an unexplained murder than he would have been if he was still breathing."

Timo walked away and faced the wall as she processed the new information.

"She's right," Cassiane said. "He could have caused any number of problems if he was still running around. Dead, he's one problem. He's a known issue. We can work around it."

"I suppose," Timo muttered.

"We've been on missions where we wish we had killed someone when we had a chance. I've never regretted pulling the trigger on anyone."

"Never?" Timo said.

Cassiane shrugged.

Timo sighed and let some of the tension out of her posture. "Okay. If this man's death becomes an issue, we can deal with it then. For now, we proceed with our current mission and forget about the hotel. Sound good?"

"I'm fine with that," Cassiane said.

Con met Cassiane's gaze and nodded her thanks. Cassiane's shrug was either a response or a dismissal. Either way, the matter was dropped.

"What is the plan?" Cassiane said.

Timo went behind the desk and pulled out the chair, wearily lowering herself into it. She pulled Rudin's papers closer and turned on the lamp.

"Now we let him sit in the darkness and silence for a while. Eventually we can take him some water, maybe something to eat. But the longer we leave him alone with his thoughts, the better it will be. He'll debate himself without us getting in the way. In the meantime, I'll see if I can work out what this letter says."

Con said, "What about us?"

"Rest. Odds are that when we finally have all the pieces of the puzzle in front of us, it will be a long time before any of us have the luxury of sleeping."

Cassiane shrugged and gestured for Con to take the couch. She went to the wall and stretched out in front of it, one arm folded under her head as a pillow. She seemed to fall asleep in the time it took Con to get to the couch and lie down. Con had to twist her head to look at Timo, whose face was cast into alternating plains of light and shadow by her desk lamp. She had opened a notebook and was busy filling a page with the alphabet so she could begin working on the code.

"Good luck."

Timo smiled. "Thank you. I'm probably going to need it."

Con smiled and relaxed, settling in. The last of her adrenaline faded, and she passed out.

CHAPTER FIFTEEN

TIMO HAD a page filled with the English and Cyrillic alphabets alongside Rudin's letter. She knew the original was most likely written by a Russian for a Russian, so she would have to decipher before she could translate. But she needed some idea of what the message said before she had any hope of cracking the code. She was passable at Russian, but she wished they had a larger team. They could have an agent who was actually adept at this sort of thing.

The words blurred in front of her again. She squeezed her eyes shut, took off her glasses, and leaned back in her seat.

"You need to sleep, too."

Timo's shoulders jumped and she looked at Cassiane. She hadn't moved, her arm still behind her head and her face concealed by shadows.

"I'll sleep."

"She's right," Con said from the couch. "Translating that note will be difficult enough without being sleep deprived. How many hours have you been awake?"

Timo put her glasses down on the desk. "Well, if no one else is asleep, how lazy will I look if I curl up for a nap? Besides, I'm not tired."

"Liar," Con said.

Timo wanted to argue that one of them needed to be awake to watch Rudin. Ideally, they would go down to open the door and make some noise so *he* couldn't get any sleep. Another perk of having a larger team. Three people just didn't cut it. She thought about the bed she had put down in the basement, the one where Cassiane had nearly died. She could picture herself sprawled out on it, a blanket pulled up to her shoulders, and felt an almost physical ache to run down and make it a reality.

She looked at the clock, just barely visible in the glow cast off from the lamp. She put down her pen and pushed away from the desk.

"Fine. For an hour."

She stepped around the desk and walked toward the file cabinet.

"Where are you going?" Con asked.

"The bed downstairs. If Rudin manages to escape and get out of the ghost station~"

Con said, "He'll find himself in a basement with no obvious exit. And if he does manage to find the ladder, we'll have enough warning to grab him when he gets into the office. If you're down there, you'll be a hostage. There's plenty of room on the couch for two."

Cassiane made a noise somewhere between a snort and a laugh. Timo was grateful the room was too dark for them to see her blush. She toed off her shoes and walked over to the couch. Con pressed herself against the back to make room, and Timo lay down on the edge. Con put one hand on Timo's waist to steady her.

"One hour," Timo said again.

Cassiane said, "I'll wake you."

Timo wanted to reiterate the time crunch, wanted to remind Cassiane that she needed sleep as well, but her eyes closed and her mind shut off in an instant. She didn't know the answer to Con's question, about how long it had been since she slept, but it had been weeks since she had a truly restful night. Her brain seized the opportunity.

She was unaware of anything until she felt a soft touch on her cheek and opened her eyes to see Cassiane staring back. Her skull was full of mothballs and all she could remember was Cassiane's injury, nursing her back to health, the joy at seeing her recover. She'd been forced to hide her joy under a mask of professional detachment, but now in this moment which felt like a dream, she could only feel relief at her friend's survival. She remembered kissing her, making love to her. Without the luxury of context, all she knew was that Cassiane had woken her up, and most likely only had one thing on her mind.

Timo acted on impulse. She cupped Cassiane's cheek and leaned forward, sliding her lips across Cassiane's mouth before pressing harder. Cassiane made a surprised sound which was muffled by their kiss. She felt fingers tightening on her hip, blunt fingernails dragged against the fabric of her pants. But something was wrong about the angle. Cassiane couldn't have scratched from front to back like that. She was aware of a weight behind her and remembered Con, was suddenly aware of where she was and how she had fallen asleep, and felt a crushing guilt close around her chest.

She broke the kiss and looked over her shoulder. Con stared back, eyes half-lidded and reflecting the lamp light. Her eyes held Timo's, moved up to Cassiane, then lowered again. No one said anything. No one moved until Con took her hand off Timo's hip and brought it up to her jaw, touching her gently to keep her from turning away as she leaned in to kiss her. Timo whimpered, then slipped her tongue against the tip of Con's.

"You were making noises in your sleep." Cassiane's voice was very quiet, her lips right next to Timo's ear. She pressed a kiss to her cheek. "I thought you were having a nightmare."

Timo brushed her lips across Con's. "You mean I'm not asleep right now?"

"No," Con said, and kissed her again.

Timo rolled onto her back and Con shifted to lie on top of her. The couch groaned as Con straddled her, and Timo realized it was because Cassiane had climbed up as well. She was sitting across Timo's legs, behind Con, arms around her as Con bent down for another kiss. Timo held her breath and kept her eyes open to watch and see what Cassiane did next. She could feel her hands moving over Con's body, working the buttons of her shirt. Timo's hands drifted up as well and slipped into the too-big shirt to feel the skin underneath.

Cassiane pulled down the suspenders to let the loops dangle. Con lifted her arms to let the sleeves of her shirt slip off, then put one arm across her chest. Cassiane took her wrist and moved it down to rest on Timo's shoulder.

"This won't work if you're shy," Cassiane scolded.

Con nodded and twisted to look over her shoulder at Cassiane, then lunged forward to kiss her. Timo held her breath as she watched, trying to decide between staring at the kiss and letting her eyes wander down Con's body. She hadn't put on a bra under the borrowed shirt, and Cassiane moved her hand up to cup one of the small breasts. The nipple seemed sharp between Cassiane's first two fingers. Timo put her hands on Con's stomach to feel the rise and fall of her breathing, sliding her fingers down to the front of her pants and fumbling to get the button open.

Con broke her kiss with Cassiane, gasping as she looked down to watch Timo. "Oh my god, what are we doing?"

Timo stilled her hands. "We can stop..."

"No," Con put a hand on her forehead, the heel of her hand against one eye. Cassiane had moved to kissing Con's neck. "No, no, no, no. I don't want that. I don't... please... don't stop... but this is so overwhelming."

Cassiane brushed her hand down the length of Con's arm, linked their fingers together, and guided it to Timo's breast. She squeezed as she went back to kissing Con's neck. Con melted under the assault.

"This isn't fair," she gasped.

"Try to enjoy it anyway." Cassiane opened her eyes and met Timo's gaze. She nodded, and Timo finished opening Con's pants. The material was baggy enough that they both could have gotten their hands inside with no trouble, but Timo wanted Con naked for this encounter. Con lowered her head and brought her legs up off the floor, and Cassiane moved so she could pull the pants off, tossing them aside before rejoining them on the couch.

Timo put her hand between Con's legs, while Con put one hand on Timo's shoulder. The other snaked around her waist, fingers splayed in the small of her back, pulling Timo to her.

"Cassiane," Timo said. "Cassiane, where are you?"

"I'm here."

Timo could see her just past Con's shoulder. Her shirt was open, revealing the patch of gauze and tape which covered her mostly-healed wound. She had pressed herself into the corner of the couch, one foot up on the cushion while the other rested on the floor. Her pants were open and her right hand was inside, the left hand cupping her own breast and teasing the nipple. She smiled, her eyes dark, and nodded at Timo.

"Keep going. You've got her right where you want her."

Timo shifted her attention to Con, who kissed her hungrily. She brushed her hand over the inside of Con's thigh and, once she accepted this was really going to happen, let muscle memory take over. She moved her hand, the fingers going to work without guidance or instruction. She lifted her head and met Con halfway for a kiss. Con dictated the rhythm by rolling her hips, hunching her shoulders, digging her knees into the cushions.

The couch protested again, and Timo felt the shift when Cassiane began moving. A moment later, she felt her own pants being undone. She moaned loud enough to be heard over Con's grunting.

"Sorry, Timothea," Cassiane said as she dragged the slacks and underwear down her muscular thighs. "I've never been good at just sitting back and watching."

Timo thought she was prepared but still cried out when she felt Cassiane's mouth on her. She thrust her hand in response and Con arched her back with a shout of surprise. Timo took advantage of Con's new position to kiss her breast, sucking the nipple into her mouth and teasing it with her teeth. She spread her legs as wide as she could with the vice grip of Con's thighs on her midsection. Cassiane used lips and tongue on her clit, fingers on her folds, and soon Timo's lower body rose to meet the touch with a mind of its own.

Con came first, her body going stiff as her hand moved to the back of Timo's head. The hair was just long enough to grab a handful of it, and Timo whispered, "It's okay, it's fine," as she moved her hand faster, fingers inside, thumb circling. Her brain was split in two, focused on what she was doing while at the same time fogged by what was being done to her. She pressed her feet against the arm of the couch and closed her eyes, baring her teeth. Con went limp and began to kiss, lick, and suck Timo's neck, hitting every erogenous spot with the flat of her tongue or the sharpness of her teeth.

Con's body was a pleasant anchor on her as Timo came. She moved her now-free hand to Con's thigh, the fingers spreading moisture across the skin. Cassiane sat up and dragged her tongue over Con's leg, licking it and Timo's wet fingers, making both of the women shudder. Con looked into Timo's eyes, breath hitching as Cassiane's tongue dipped between her legs. She wet her lips and then kissed Timo hard, passionately. Timo didn't know if Con came a second time or if Cassiane had just caused an aftershock, but either way, she reveled in the way Con shook.

Timo kissed Con's temple. "Are you okay, Constance?"

Con nodded and burrowed her face against Timo's shoulder.

The couch shifted as Cassiane stood up. Timo and Con both turned their heads to watch as she undressed with her back to them. Timo was always impressed with Cassiane's body. She was transfixed by the way her muscles moved, and now the sheen of sweat on her skin reflected the lamp light and made every flex and bulge look like it was electrified. As she stepped out of her trousers, Con pushed up and stepped off the couch as if in a trance. Cassiane twisted at the waist to watch her approach.

"You don't have to do anything," Cassiane said. "I can get by just watching. I like watching."

Con circled Cassiane, standing in front of her, holding her gaze. She brought a hand to her mouth, licked the fingers, and reached between Cassiane's legs. Cassiane inhaled through her teeth and clenched her teeth. Timo rolled onto her side and rested her head on one hand. The other hand went to her lap, stroking the skin that was still wet from Cassiane's tongue. She exhaled softly as she watched what was unfolding in front of her.

"You can get by?" Con said. "When have you ever been okay with just 'getting by,' Miss Jurick?" She began to move her hand.

Cassiane grunted and swayed on her feet.

Timo rolled off the couch. Her own knees were untrustworthy as she took the two steps required to take her to the other woman. She pressed against Cassiane from behind, hands on her shoulders, and kissed her hair.

"Just relax," Timo said. "Put your weight on me."

Con leaned in and kissed Cassiane. Timo moved one hand down to cup Cassiane's breasts, supporting her.

"Is she very wet?" Timo whispered.

"Very wet," Con confirmed. "Look…"

She brought her hand up, and Timo took two fingers into her mouth. She moved her hand down so Cassiane wouldn't feel neglected, rubbing her, feeling the wetness for herself. Con pressed against Cassiane from in front, pinning her between their bodies, and kissed Timo's lips. Cassiane moved her head to bite Con's shoulder, one hand swinging back and grabbing Timo's waist, pulling her forward.

Timo was lightheaded. Her mind branched off in a dozen directions, things she wanted to do and taste and feel. She tasted Cassiane on Con's fingers. When Con twisted her neck and kissed Cassiane, Timo knew they were sharing her taste, and she could see flashes of their tongues as she pushed two fingers deep into

Cassiane, thrusting her hips symbolically against the curve of Cassiane's ass.

At some point, they ended up on the ground. There were moments when two of them focused on each other while the third watched, and other moments where Timo was kissing a body part without knowing which of her new lovers it belonged to. Names were passionately whispered against heated skin, sweat and spit and other fluids spread over mouths and fingers.

Eventually Con begged relief, twisting away from them to lie on her stomach. She put her head down on crossed arms, heaved a heavy breath, and passed out. Timo and Cassiane exchanged a look, then Cassiane crawled to the couch. She came back with the cushions and their discarded clothes, and Timo helped her arrange a nest. They decided without speaking to flank Con, Timo's hand on her shoulder and Cassiane's in the small just above the curve of her rear. They looked at each other across the mountain range of Con's shoulders.

"You really were making noises in your sleep," Cassiane whispered.

Timo nodded. "I believe you."

Cassiane moved her thumb back and forth over a dimple in Con's back. "It was because she was touching you."

Timo smiled. Her eyelids were getting heavy again. "I know. She was asleep, too. She didn't mean to do it. I don't think she's used to sleeping next to people."

"I just didn't want to lie there and watch."

"I thought you could get by with watching."

"Sometimes," Cassiane said. Then again, softer, "Sometimes."

Timo smiled and closed her eyes while Cassiane was still staring at her, and assumed she was still staring when she joined Con in sleep.

CHAPTER SIXTEEN

RUDIN'S CHIN was on his chest when Timo opened the door to the ghost station, but his head snapped up so quickly it might have been attached to the handle by some kind of pulley system. He squinted at her and blinked when she turned on the lights. The stubble on his cheeks had darkened in the short time he'd been their prisoner. Judging by the smell, he had also soiled himself. She was disgusted but kept herself from giving off any outward signs that she even noticed.

"You have a choice, Mr. Rudin." She stood in front of him, hands behind her back. "Food. Water. Cigarette. You can only have one for free. You can purchase the other two by answering one of our questions. What itch requires the most immediate scratching?"

He spit on the tile in front of her feet. "Save your charity. I want nothing from you."

Timo sighed and rolled her head back on her shoulders. "We'll see how you feel in a few hours." When she looked at him again, she caught him looking at her wrists. He averted his gaze quickly but it was clear he had been looking for a watch. "Curious about how long you've been down here? Less than a day, you think, but was it a full night? Is it morning or afternoon? Is the sun up yet?" She bent at the waist to put her face closer to his. "Has the deadline passed?"

Rudin met her gaze. "You look tired, woman. Perhaps you had a very long night worrying about your failure."

She smiled. "I had a fantastic evening, Mr. Rudin. My sincere hope is that we wrap this nonsense up quickly so I can continue having good nights that don't involve having a man tied up in my basement. I've wasted far too much of my time and energy to you, to this mission, and I am eager for it to be over. I cannot wait until I never have to think about you ever again, Pavel Rudin."

He grunted and broke eye contact first. Timo straightened and walked away from him.

"I believe that unless we stop it, there is going to be an attack. My people will recognize it when it happens. They will see how anthrax could have been used, or they will connect the culprits to this city or to you, and they will know it is the mission we failed to stop. They will know you could have stopped it. When the time comes to retaliate, they will want to make you suffer. Your home. Your loved ones. People who have nothing to do with any of this will suffer."

Rudin's jaw was trembling. There was a tremor in his fingers.

"Is it worth their lives, Pavel? Let's just end this. Let the mission fail, let them go back to the drawing board. End this battle so the war can grind on."

"It's not just one battle," he muttered. "If it was just one battle... you have no idea what is at stake. The days of holding guns to each other's heads is over."

Timo stared at him as she processed his words, dissecting them in her mind. It took her a moment, but then she understood.

"This is a demonstration."

Rudin met her gaze again.

"Whatever is going to happen is a show of strength. To prove that the Soviet Union is strong, to make its enemies afraid. But... anyone can make anthrax, so that's not it. The delivery system?" She was looking through Rudin at this point. The gears in her mind were turning. "The people you were supposed to meet need the anthrax because it was the bullet in their gun. The gun is what's important. They have a weapon which could disperse the anthrax in a way that would make the Soviet Union look strong. What is it? A bomb?"

Rudin shook his head from side to side. "Waste all the time you want. It's not going to matter in the end. People will die on both sides. It's the way the world has to be."

"It's the way you've chosen to make the world, Pavel. That is the choice you're making right now in this room, between the two of us. I want to stop deaths. I want to make retaliation against your people unnecessary." Her voice had slowly rose until she was practically screaming. "I want *peace*, goddamn it, and your silence is ensuring death and devastation. That blood is going to be on your hands."

"I chose to come here." He was subdued now. "I knew what I made, I knew what they wanted it for, and I made the decision to come here and give it to them. Of course the blood is on my hands, woman. I accepted that before I even left home. You think I'm simply evil, a monster who wants to sow chaos for chaos' sake. I don't want that any more than you do. I don't hate the people who will die. They're a means to an end. Maybe that makes me evil. I just want my country and my people to survive. I don't want them to be crushed and blown away into dust. The Americans or whoever you work for, the British or the Italians or whoever... you cloak yourselves as history's heroes. We dare to diverge from your path and we're called monsters, villains. How many appalling, inhuman things are in your history? How many lives were lost so that *your* country survived?"

Timo didn't dare look away from him.

"So you try to shame me by saying their blood is on my hands? Fine. I doubt I'll notice it with all the blood that is already there."

She kept her voice steady. "We've decided that your meeting was supposed to take place before sunset tonight. Just an educated guess on our part. But if you haven't given us what we need by then, it's unlikely you ever will. So no matter what, you will have exhausted your use to us. So we'll bring your anthrax in here and expose you to it. You won't receive medical attention, so your death is certain to be agonizing. It's only fair considering that you intended to make countless others suffer the same fate. Maybe they'll find your body down here someday when they open the station again. Maybe not. This is where the story of Pavel Rudin ends."

He smiled grimly and looked around. "It's certainly a unique end. Better than what I had planned. You must have deduced I was never going back to Dubna. I was going to hand over the spores and then I would go home and put a bullet in my brain. Do you think I want to be around to see the newspapers? To see the weeping faces on newspapers and watch the dead count rise? What I'm doing is not for me, it's for future generations."

"Future generations who won't exist," Timo said sadly, "because this fire we keep stoking will eventually burn the ground so thoroughly that nothing can grow. Neither side will win in the end. All that will be left is a husk."

She walked to the door and, this time, left the light on.

"Enjoy your final day, Mr. Rudin. And consider my offer. Food, water, cigarette. You can still have one for free."

She shut the door on him.

Cassiane was seated at Dr. Lippert's desk, bent over the note, attempting to find patterns. Con sat in the patient's chair and watched her. She'd woken up on the floor between Cassiane and Timo, the three of them lined up like spoons in a drawer. It was so perfect and so surreal that she thought she must have been dreaming. She kept her cheek against Cassiane's shoulder until she felt Timo's fingers tighten slightly on her hip, then drag higher before it stopped.

"Oh, shit..."

Those were the only two words spoken about the previous night's event. Timo got up, dressed, and immediately descended into the basement where she was presumably having a conversation with Rudin. Con had put on her own clothes again and retreated, reluctantly leaving Cassiane to wake up on the floor naked and alone. If she was offended or confused when she finally woke, she didn't give it away. She simply gathered the clothes on which she'd been sleeping, pulled on a shirt and slacks, and sat down behind the desk.

It had been an hour, and Con finally couldn't take the silence any longer. "I'm surprised you slept longer than we did."

Cassiane kept examining the note. "Never pass up a chance for sleep, slop, or screwing. I learned that a long time ago."

"Slop?"

"Food. Eating."

"Oh."

"There was no immediate threat and no reason to get up at the crack of dawn, so I slept as much as I could in case tomorrow is different. I eat whenever food is offered to me because I don't know when the next meal is coming from."

"You fuck whoever is willing because why not?"

This time Cassiane looked up. She held Con's gaze and then looked down again. "Not really. I can go a long time without screwing anyone, really. Usually it doesn't come up."

"I've never had sex on a mission before."

"It can get in the way," Cassiane said. "But it can also help. Bonding. Stress relief. It really comes down to the people involved."

Con thought about that until Timo returned from the basement. She looked between the two of them, then decided to focus on the note.

"Have you made any progress?"

Cassiane nodded and tapped the note. "This part here. These aren't words."

Con sat up straighter. Timo moved closer to the desk and said, "How can you tell?"

Cassiane pointed. "Punctuation here and here. That's not a period, it's a decimal point. There's a second string here. They both have hash marks at the end. Degrees. These are satellite coordinates. Two digits in front of the decimal, six after them."

"So the letters correspond with numbers?" Timo's shoulders sagged. "Shit."

"It's not as hopeless as it sounds," Cassiane said, "but it's still... vaguely hopeless. The latitude and longitude have to be 52 and 13."

Con said, "Why?"

"Because..." Cassiane made a gesture with her hands. "They just have to be. It could be 52 and 12, but then the two integers next to the decimal would be the same. They're different, so that means it has to be 13. You'd have to go too far away from Berlin for the numbers to change that much. So if we know this number is a 5, this is 2, this is 1, and this is 3..."

"We might be able to find the full coordinates." Timo sounded excited now. She pulled her notebook to her side of the desk and craned her neck to see the section Cassiane had been talking about. "How many digits do you need to narrow it down?"

"Get as many as you can," Cassiane said, "but I don't need all of them. Get a majority and it show us a general area."

Con watched Timo examine the list she'd just made. "How long will this take you?"

"I don't know," Timo muttered. She chewed on her thumbnail, her eyes narrowing. "There's a pattern. I can't see it yet. One through three, and then five... it's not a straight alphabetical cypher..."

"Before you get too far into that," Con said, "did you learn anything from Rudin this morning?"

"Whatever his companions have planned, it's supposed to serve as a show of strength." She sounded distracted, like someone explaining what she'd had for breakfast. "Some kind of weapon. I believe the anthrax was going to be delivered in a new way."

"Bomb?" Cassiane asked.

"Not a bomb," Timo said. "Probably not. I don't think bomb, didn't... I-I didn't think he was talking about a bomb." She rubbed a finger across her eyebrow, bumping her glasses a little further down her nose. "Some other large-scale delivery system."

"Maybe a patient zero," Con said. "Rudin was supposed to meet someone here, infect them, and then that person would walk onto the London Underground or Times Square and just start coughing."

"Sh," Timo said, still distracted. "This could be four... no, that doesn't..." She scratched that out.

Cassiane stood up. "I can confirm what the method is."

Timo snapped back to attention. "Circe, no. If we get false information from him at this point, we could lose valuable time."

"We've already lost most of the time we had. I'm just going to confirm our theory."

"No. I'm not confident enough in it to take the risk."

Cassiane started to protest, but Timo slashed the air with her pencil.

"We're not forcing any information from him! Get out of here. You're distracting me. Go for a walk. Change into some clean clothes, get some breakfast. Get us all some breakfast."

Con reached across the desk and put her hand on top of Cassiane's. Timo and Cassiane both looked at it, but neither said anything. She spoke calmly, soothingly. "He knows we're running out of time. Violence will only look like desperation to him. If you go down and start punching him, he'll know we're grasping at straws and his incentive to help us will evaporate."

Timo said, "She's right."

Cassiane took a deep breath and let it out slowly. She slipped her hand out from underneath Con's and walked away from the desk.

"Fine. But the time will come when we have to cross that line, when we'll be desperate enough we won't have a choice but to show our cards. And it's approaching faster than either of you want to admit." She picked up her coat and pulled it on as she walked to the door.

"Where are you going?" Timo asked.

"Breakfast."

The door slammed behind her. Timo sighed, hung her head, and then went back to decoding the coordinates from the note.

CHAPTER SEVENTEEN

RUDIN LIFTED his head long enough to see who was joining him, smiling when he saw Cassiane. "Ah, Circe. Good. Maybe I can convince you to put an end to all of this. You seem like the sort of woman who could kill someone with your bare hands. Why not save everyone some time and do it? I'd prefer not to provoke you into it, but I think I could~"

She dropped a map on the floor in front of him. Timo had drawn a red circle around a wooded area not far from Berlin. Rudin stared at it, the false humor evaporating from his face. He went pale, and beads of sweat appeared on his brow.

"What is that?"

"That's what I came in here to ask you, Mr. Rudin. It looks like forest to me, but I think it's something far more sinister." Cassiane crouched on the other side of the map and stabbed the center of the circle with her finger. "Is that where your friends are waiting? Hm? Do they have a bunker? How many of them are there? What sort of security should we expect?"

He glared at her. "I don't know what a forest has to do with anything."

She grinned. "Of course you do, Pavel. You can lie all you want, but your body gave you away. You didn't expect to see this map. You certainly didn't expect this area to be marked. You wanted me to put an end to this. You can put an end to it."

"Go to hell."

Cassiane stood up and fished in her pocket. She withdrew a cigarette and placed it in her mouth, lighting it with a matchstick. "This can all be over for you right now. Tell us what is in the forest. We will go and take care of them. Then we'll come back and let you go."

He laughed, but it was a sick sound. His eyes were locked on the smoke trailing from her lips. He looked like a caged animal who had been denied food. "Yes, I believe that will definitely happen. The housekeeper and the backpacker. And the, the other one. The maybe blonde one who has never come in here to speak to me, but I saw her too. I've seen all your faces too well for you to ever let me go."

"Maybe those aren't the only two options. Maybe you decide to cooperate with us, come back home, tell our superiors all your dirty little secrets. No more unnecessary deaths on either side."

"You want me to turn traitor."

"When this is all said and done, will your people really believe you didn't talk? Will they trust you ever again? This could be the end of your career or just the beginning of its next step."

Rudin shook his head. "This is not a real offer. The woman with the glasses wouldn't have sent you in to make this offer. She would have sent the blonde. A new face, maybe someone who is more reasonable. Not my interrogator, not the rough one, but a potential ally. You are here to see what my reaction is." He sighed. "Just end this."

Cassiane blew a line of smoke out to one side. "What's in the forest?"

Rudin was visibly tense, either from the sight of her cigarette or the smell. "Nothing."

"What is in the forest."

"A fucking battalion armed to the teeth just waiting to rip you apart."

Cassiane said, "Life as you know it is over. You never planned to leave Berlin. You have a chance to stay alive. I'm the one making the offer so you will understand that it isn't mercy or pity. It's not a kindness. You will be an employee who is only useful as long as you continue helping us. I am your reminder that there will always be a sword dangling above your head waiting for its cord to be cut, and I am going to be the person cutting the cord."

He held her gaze. "I think you are conflicted. Or rather, the other woman is. She knows something will have to be done with me when this is all over. She knows she can't set me free but she doesn't have the guts to murder me in cold blood. You say this offer isn't mercy? It is. Just not for me. It's mercy for your friends out there who can't bear the thought of having my blood on their hands."

She picked up the map and carefully refolded it.

"You seem to be under the mistaken impression this is our first assignment. You look at us and see schoolgirls who wouldn't know how to hold a gun even if we figured out how to load it. So let me tell you something about my friend with the glasses. What did we decide to call her, Medea? I like that name. It's fitting. This is a story about her actual first mission.

"She was in charge of a small team. Four agents. It was supposed to be a quick intelligence gathering mission, but something went wrong. A cover was blown, two members of the team were taken into custody and one was fatally wounded making his escape. Medea was left with one team member safe and two captured by the enemy. Just like you."

She was pacing now, casually punctuating every few sentences with a drag from her cigarette. The map was folded under her arm. Timo had told her this story herself, and Cassiane had heard enough details from other sources to confirm it was true.

"Medea had a decision to make. She could scrub the mission, take the surviving team member home, chalk it up as a failure. Or she could get the information they'd been sent there to find and rescue her fellow agents. She could turn it into a win. But it would be a great risk."

Rudin sighed. "And she found a brilliant way to infiltrate the station house, free her men, and get the information without being caught."

"In a way," Cassiane said. "She walked through the front door and shot every fucking face she saw. Even she doesn't know how many people she killed. Some people say eight, others say twelve. You see, I can cause pain in people. I can make people hurt. Medea is different because when that moment comes, she stops seeing them as people. She sees them as problems. Problems can be solved by a bullet. Part of her mind shuts off. The compassionate side, maybe, I don't know, it just goes away. That's her talent. She solves problems. And if the solution leaves the floor a little bloody, then she can live with that."

Rudin worked his jaw, still staring at her, but she could see a twitch at the corner of one eye.

"Think about it. Oh." She looked at the cigarette as if she'd forgotten about it. She held it up so he could see. "Medea told me the offer still stands. Food. Water. Cigarette. You get one for free. Have you decided?"

"Go to hell."

Cassiane nodded and dropped the cigarette on the floor. She didn't bother to snuff it as she stepped out of the room.

"That wasn't true," Timo said once the door was closed. Even so, she kept her voice low so it couldn't pass through to Rudin's ears. She was hugging herself, eyes down and cast in shadows.

"Of course it was," Cassiane said. "I saw the photographs myself. You went through the building like an avenging angel."

"The story is true," Timo admitted, "but you said no one knows how many people I killed. I know. I can't stop thinking about it. There were seven. One woman, six men. Three of the men had mustaches, one had glasses. One of the men without mustaches wept when he saw me coming. The last words of the last man I killed were 'do you think I won't kill a woman'. The woman was beautiful. Redheaded. She looked angry when I killed her."

Cassiane listened in respectful silence. When Timo held out her hand, Cassiane gave her the map.

"Don't tell that story again. Or, if you must... don't exaggerate."

"Seven," Cassiane repeated.

Timo nodded and took the ladder back up to the office.

Con came back into the office to find Timo and Cassiane seated in their respective chairs, the perfect image of therapist and patient. She had gone back to her rooms to change into clean clothes, and she'd brought extra outfits for them. Cassiane suggested dark colors just in case they ended up going into the forest. Con put the bag down on the desk and turned to face them with her arms crossed over her chest. She waited for them to speak first, then gave up.

"I assume he didn't give up any new information."

Timo shook her head. "He's still not taking us up on the rewards."

"It would be different if we had more time," Cassiane said. "He's been trained as well as we have. It will be a few hours yet before food and water would be enough to make him crack."

"We don't have hours," Timo said.

"I know." Cassiane sighed. "Cigarettes had a better chance. He's obviously stressed and in withdrawal. It must be anguish to give up the chance to have a smoke."

Con said, "The withdrawal is feeding him. He feels as if he deserves the pain."

"Hm," Timo said thoughtfully, then shook her head. She stood up and moved to stand between the other two women. "I don't believe we're going to make any progress with him. At least not in the time left. Our only option is to see what those coordinates point to. It will at least give us some idea about how to proceed. If it's a secret base, we'll know we're up against an army. If it's a cabin, we can assume it's a smaller force. I'll go."

"I should be the one who goes," Con said. "Intelligence is my job."

Timo said, "This isn't intelligence gathering. It's orienteering while remaining inconspicuous. Once I see what's there, I can decide on the next step. Planning. That's *my* job."

They both looked at Cassiane as if expecting her to make an argument as well. She shrugged.

"You two are the brains. I'll go when you need muscle."

"Fine," Con said. "We'll stay here and watch over him. But be careful. And if you haven't come back in three hours, we'll come after you."

Timo said, "You can't leave Rudin unguarded."

"We'll break Rudin's ankles and then come after you."

Timo actually managed to smile at that. "Fair enough." She nodded at the bag Con had brought in with her. "Did you bring dark clothes?"

"I did. Turtleneck and slacks. I had a pair of heavy shoes, for the terrain, but I'm not sure if they will fit you..."

"It will be fine." She took the bag and walked toward the ladder.

"Where are you going?" Cassiane said.

Timo looked confused. "To change clothes."

Cassiane raised an eyebrow. "Shy?"

"I'm... I just thought..."

Cassiane said, "It was pretty dark in here last night, but I think everyone in this room can give up the idea of modesty."

Con blushed bright red, looking at her shoes.

Timo slowly faced them again. "Okay... I suppose maybe we

should talk about what happened here last night." No one spoke up, so she held her hands out. "Or we can just pretend it never happened and move on."

"No," Con said, then shyly retreated. "I-I mean, it was wonderful. It was something I'd never experienced. I never thought I'd want to experience. But I don't want to pretend it was a dream."

Timo said, "Neither do I. But I think we can all agree that our current circumstances aren't the best in which to explore the situation. We'll wrap up this mission and then, when the dust settles, we'll have a conversation. Does that work for everyone?"

Con nodded. Cassiane, who had been silent, gave an indifferent shrug.

"Cassiane?"

"I would be happy if it happened again," she said, "but I probably wouldn't shed any tears if I never saw either of you again outside of Berlin. I don't mean to sound cold. Last night was probably one of the best nights I've ever had. Timo, the nights you and I shared alone are in the running for the top spot as well. But I've never put a personal relationship before my work and I don't intend to start now. I know that sounds cold, but it's how I feel."

Timo said, "Fair enough, I suppose." She put her covert outfit down on the desk and pulled her shirt over her head so she could change.

Con looked away, surrendering to modesty despite the conversation they'd just had, and that was how she saw that Cassiane was also looking at the floor. For all her bluster and denials, it seemed as if she was more emotionally involved than she wanted to admit. Con smiled at the realization and looked away from Cassiane as well, giving both women their privacy.

CHAPTER EIGHTEEN

THE BACKSEAT of the car still had blood on the upholstery from Cassiane's near-death, but Timo had covered it with a blanket and a pile of coats to prevent anyone from spotting it with a cursory glance. It was the best she could do under their current circumstances. The map was unfolded in the seat beside her, with a route drawn by Con. It would be nearly impossible to explain if she was caught with it, but the woods were difficult enough to navigate when using the roads. The coordinates pointed to a spot which seemed to be in the middle of nowhere, and she didn't want to risk getting lost or turned around.

As she drove, she tried to keep her mind clear but it kept going back to the story Cassiane had told. She hated that other agents knew it, was irritated that Cassiane used it the way she had, and absolutely despised knowing that others had probably used it the same way. She'd done what needed to be done. She would do it again. But she would never be the same person she was before pulling the trigger. She didn't think she would even recognize that girl.

That was just one of the reasons she envied Cassiane. She knew Cassiane wasn't a robot, but the woman could process violence in a way that made her perfect for this job. Probably not the best person to enter into a romantic relationship with, though...

Timo had no idea what she was thinking on that mark. Sleeping with an agent wasn't exactly sanctioned, but she personally frowned upon it. She found it complicated things far too much to be worth the trouble. Then Cassiane happened. Then Con... God, how had she let that happen? If sleeping with Cassiane was foolish, sleeping with Con was downright self-destructive. And sleeping with both of them...

She had been driving as her mind worked through the maze of complicated emotions, checking the map to follow its route without thought. Now she realized she was nearing a fork in the road and slowed down, checking for landmarks that would help her know when to stop. Con had chosen a point where Timo could park and walk in a straight line to the coordinates. It was by no means an exact map - none of them had ever been on this road before, and they could only trust the map's accuracy to a certain degree - so she would have to guess a little.

The road on the map curved to avoid a small hill so, when the land began to rise on the southern side of her car, she pulled into the grass. She took the map, her camera, and a compass, tucked a revolver into her belt, and ascended the short hill. A barbed-wire fence attempted to block her from going further, but she used her boot to hold down one end as she slipped through. She paused to make sure she hadn't snagged any of her clothes, and marched onward into the wild.

She expected to be wading through overgrowth, but the grass was remarkably tamed. In some places the weeds whipped at her knees, and she had to keep a wary eye out for snakes, but for the most part it was no different than walking through someone's untended backyard. The trees were skeletal, their white trunks twisting and turning into frozen cobwebs high above her head. Stiff pine needles scraped the sleeves of her jacket and threatened to scratch hashmarks on her cheeks when she didn't duck quickly enough.

The compass kept her on a true path, even though she occasionally had to detour around stones or particularly large trees. She stopped only once to catch her breath and take a drink of water before she arrived at the X on her map. The trees were widely-spaced enough that she could see there was nothing in the immediate vicinity, so she continued forward at a slower pace. Twigs snapped underfoot and she could hear nothing but birdsong overhead.

Timo was close to admitting defeat when she saw a wall of grey ahead of her. At first she thought it was a natural stone formation, but the line where it cut through the grass was too uniform to be anything but man-made. She crouched and listened but couldn't hear any sounds of anyone else in the area. She gave it a full minute before she determined there weren't any soldiers nearby and stood up again. Now that she was looking at it, she saw the wall was only about fifteen feet high. She couldn't see where the wall ended, but it appeared to be smooth and unbroken on this side.

She considered circling to find the entrance but didn't want to risk running into guards. She looked at the trees nearby and noticed all branches at ground level had been sawn or broken off to prevent anyone from easily climbing them. Fortunately, she had spent a good amount of childhood years climbing trees and didn't see this as an insurmountable problem. She backtracked until she found a tree with a low enough branch, secured her supplies, and hauled herself up. From there she went up another level, then a third. Standing on that branch, a good two meters off the ground, she examined the next tree over and took a leap. Her boot kicked off a little bark, and she had to cling to the trunk for dear life until she regained her balance, but she managed to not fall. The bark was like tiny knives under her fingers, sharp enough to stab the tender skin before shattering to mulch and tumbling to the ground in a storm of wooden hail.

The next tree was almost out of her range, but she managed to land that one as well. She climbed higher, where the branches overlapped more so she could go from one tree to the next as easily as using stepping stones. She still had to use the trunks for balance but the risk of falling diminished the higher she got. Her main danger came from a startled squirrel who raced across her foot chittering at her violation of his space.

Soon she was close enough to see over the wall. From this height, she could see broken glass embedded in mortar on top of the wall to deter anyone from climbing over. She had no intention of getting inside, not on his trip. She just wanted to see what was waiting for them. She crouched down and put her shoulder against the trunk to let it take her weight. With her free hand, she brought up the camera and began to take pictures of the fortress.

The wall enclosed a space about the size of a city block. She saw an entrance on the north side, to her left, but no other access points. A sedan was parked behind the closed door as if it was waiting to head out for a grocery run. There were two prefab buildings: an unremarkable white square she assumed served as barracks against the west side of the space, and a steel A-frame garage on the south. In the center of the space was a helicopter, its blades covered with camouflage netting like a handkerchief draped over a lamp. She didn't know helicopter models, but it was a big one. She imagined it could hold more than five troops, maybe as many as ten. Arms stuck out from either side of the chopper, long wings with barrel-like attachments hanging from the underside.

Timo took pictures of it all, including the security, but saved a few exposures in case anyone made an appearance. She saw no sign of patrolling guards, but there might be measures she couldn't see. The cleared space around the entrance could be booby-trapped with landmines. She remained where she was, confident the canopy concealed her even if someone in the fortress came outside and looked up. The sweat she'd worked up during the hike and her climb evaporated as she waited. She moved the camera to her coat pocket so her hand wouldn't cramp from holding it.

Intelligence officers always wanted to be in the field. They scraped and fought for field assignments, dreading the prison of desk work. But the truth was so much field work was spent just like this, sore and tired and miserable and trying not to fall out of a tree while staring at a door which may or may not open. She would trade this for a climate-controlled office and swivel chair in a heartbeat. And a desk where she could lay her head for a quick mid-morning nap. And a bottom drawer with a cache of sweets. She imagined biting into a pasteli bar and her mouth watered.

Her mind had blurred out the unchanging picture in front of her until suddenly it changed, and Timo blinked her eyes back into focus. The door to the barracks had opened and a man emerged. He wore uniform pants but only a white undershirt, his tattooed arms exposed as he walked briskly toward the sedan. He was tall with close-cropped blonde hair. He looked like the caveman from a cartoon she used to watch, so she named him Barney in her head. She took a picture of his profile.

He walked to the car and opened the passenger door. He pulled out a notebook, opened it on the car's roof, and made a note of something with a pen which he'd produced from his pocket. Timo snapped a photo of his face. It would be blurry to the point of being a complete smear but, at this distance, she couldn't hope for much. Barney finished writing and put the book back into the sedan.

Someone else had come out of the barracks. He was dressed like a thousand other Berlin residents - unbuttoned work shirt, white tank top, dungarees - and his black hair shone with pomade. He had a thick brush of a mustache and she decided he looked like Freddy Mercury with a wider build.

"Fred and Barney," she muttered with a smile.

Barney walked back and the men spoke. She could hear their voices well enough to believe they were speaking Russian. Fred spoke, Barney replied, and Fred grimaced and looked at the ground. He spoke again and Barney nodded. Fred stepped aside so Barney could go back into the barracks. Once he was gone, Fred took a few more steps away from the building and withdrew a pack of cigarettes from his pocket. Timo took photos of him as he lit up and took a drag.

Barney was only gone long enough to change into an outfit similar to Fred's. He was carrying something which caught the light and glinted brightly: car keys.

"Shit," Timo muttered. He was going to drive the sedan out of this fortress, and whatever road he used would likely take him past the place where she had left her car. Her brain put all of this together as her body was already in the process of climbing down the tree. She couldn't take the time to backtrack across the branches so she was going to have to take a fall.

The lowest branch on this tree was about two and a half meters off the ground. She sat down to let her legs dangle, turned around, gripped the branch and dropped down. She rolled as soon as she landed but the shock still transferred up through her legs and into her spine like a sharp jolt of electricity. Her adrenaline let her ignore it for the time being, and she broke into a sprint.

She hadn't seen the road coming out of the fortress, but the road on which she was parked was to the east. There was a chance Barney would emerge from the woods too far north to pass her. But she still wanted to follow him if it was at all possible. He might be setting out to meet Rudin. So she ran, ignoring the pain in her legs and back, making sure she had her camera and weapon as she ducked branches and leapt over fallen logs, forgoing any care she had taken on her journey into the woods.

In her haste, she forgot about the barbed wire and tried to squirm through. It cut through her sleeve, slicing the skin in one line from her right wrist to elbow and another near her left shoulder. She cursed and threw herself behind the wheel of the car. She felt the blood under her clothes and the increasing sting of her cuts, but she couldn't waste time tending to them. The car was parked in the wrong direction so she reversed into the grass, praying she didn't puncture the tires on any stones or sticks, and aimed it back toward Berlin.

She looked down every side road she passed, expecting to see the sedan on all of them, but it didn't appear until she was almost back in the city. Barney pulled out in front of her without slowing down or looking back, so she was forced to step on the brakes or tap his bumper with hers. She was shocked but still leaned out the window and shouted an obscenity at him as if she was just another motorist. Barney didn't even bother looking back as he sped on.

Timo followed.

CHAPTER NINETEEN

AFTER TIMO left, Cassiane stretched out on the couch to get some sleep. She saw no need to speak with Rudin again, and she got the impression Con wanted to talk more about the night before. When she woke, not entirely certain of how much time had passed, Con was seated behind Timo's desk with Rudin's coded letter in front of her. She wrote something in her notebook, looked at Cassiane, then went back to her work. Cassiane sat up and swung her feet down onto the floor.

"Any word from Timo?"

"Not yet," Con said. "I'm not making much progress on this mess, either."

Cassiane stood. "We could make Rudin tell us what it says."

"I doubt he'd be willing to help us."

"I don't plan to give him much of a choice. We know where the coordinates lead. If Timo finds something useful there, we may no longer have any reason to keep him around. We can stop worrying about whether or not he ever leaves that room."

Con looked up at Cassiane, examining her for a long moment before speaking. "Who are you?"

"You know who I am. Cassiane Jurick. Circe. Sophie Rasch. The late Marta Gresham."

"Not your cover identities, and not even your name. I mean, when you aren't on assignment, when you go home and have downtime to relax. Who is Cassiane Jurick then?"

Cassiane was thrown by the question but tried not to show it. "She's... an agent waiting to be told where she needs to go. Learning what she needs to know to become someone else. Languages. Skills."

"But what are your *hobbies?*"

"I just told you."

Con laughed without humor and shook her head. "That can't be true. You're not a machine. You aren't a tool that's just sitting in a shed waiting for someone to come use you."

Cassiane said, "It's what I'm good at."

"Don't you have partners? Lovers?"

"That would be cruel, don't you think?"

Con furrowed her brow. "How so?"

"I wouldn't be able to tell her anything about what I do. I couldn't give her mission details. And then I would vanish for weeks at a time, maybe months, with no explanation. Then I would come back with bullet wounds and scars which I also couldn't explain. Why would I do that to someone?"

"Oh." Con clearly hadn't considered it from that angle.

"You can always have trysts," Cassiane said. "The human body needs comfort and contact from time to time or we go mad. But commitment is a luxury we can't hope for."

Con said, "I always imagined settling down with somebody one day."

Cassiane shrugged. "We'll always need people back at the home office."

"I love the field..."

"Then you'll need to compromise something," Cassiane said. "It may sound harsh, but it's what we all have to do in our business. You can't do work like this without giving up something vital."

Con looked down at the note framed by her hands. Cassiane felt a twinge of guilt for ruining the girl's mood, but she wouldn't apologize for telling the truth. It might have been harsh but it was something she needed to be told. She rounded the desk and stood behind the chair, placing her hands on Con's shoulders. She began kneading the muscles with her fingers.

"There are benefits to the sacrifice. What happened last night would have been impossible if any of us had someone waiting at home. Don't count what you might have one day. Only count the things you actually have in your grasp."

"Hm." Con nodded and covered Cassiane's right hand with

her left. "That is very good advice. Thank you."

Cassiane moved her hand down to cup Con's breast through her blouse, bending her knees so the other hand could travel lower. Con tensed and looked down to watch as the fingers spread out over the crotch of her trousers. The new position put her lips next to Con's ear so she could lower her voice.

"If I had someone at home, I wouldn't be able to do this. And if *you* had someone, you'd have to tell me to stop. Do you want to tell me to stop?"

Con swallowed hard and shook her head 'no.' She was tense in the chair, her hands still up by her shoulders. Her fingers had curled into loose fists. Cassiane kissed her neck and began to move the hand between Con's legs. Con moved her hips in response, pressing back against the chair so that it creaked. Cassiane smiled and focused on rubbing her.

"I've always found this to be a fun part of the missions."

"You... d-do th-this a lot?"

Cassiane said, "Not a lot. Sometimes. Never with men. You give men a little bit of attention and they'll think they're entitled to your everything." Her lips were moving against the collar of Con's shirt as she spoke. She moved her chin so they touched her skin instead. "Women understand it's a little more give and take."

"But you have been with men before?"

"When I have to be. I wouldn't recommend it."

Con shifted. "I think I would like it. Not... I-I mean, I have been with men before, but it... it was over so quickly. I never had much of a chance to form an opinion. And even though I f-felt like this for women, I never thought it was a real option, so I didn't let myself... What I mean is, I think I could be happy with either... I've always thought that made me strange."

"Maybe so," Cassiane said. "Stand up and take off your pants."

Con looked back to see Cassiane was already rising. "What's... what..."

"I'm going to demonstrate something for you."

She did as she was told, and Cassiane pushed the chair out of the way. Con looked at the door.

"Should we... I mean, now... it's the middle of the day..."

"Then we should be quiet."

Con looked at the door again, then unbuttoned her pants. Cassiane waited until she was pushing them down to put a hand on her shoulder and spin her around. She pushed Con down onto the desk and crowded up behind her, pressing their hips together. Both of Con's arms were pinned underneath her at first, but she was able to push herself up onto her elbows.

"This is men." Cassiane gripped Con's hip with one hand while she pressed the other between Con's legs. Con gasped, hunching her shoulders as Cassiane rubbed her roughly with two fingers. "Doesn't care if you're wet, doesn't care if you're comfortable, just worries about getting what he needs." She pushed her fingers inside. Con cried out and put her head down on the desk as Cassiane began thrusting.

Con turned her head so Cassiane couldn't see her face. After a moment she stretched out both arms and gripped the far edge of the desk. She moved her feet apart and began pushing back against Cassiane's hand. Cassiane tightened her fingers on the soft skin of Con's hip and watched her shoulders carefully.

"You like this?" Cassiane asked.

Con moaned and put her forehead down on the desk. She said, "Don't stop," which was probably easier than just saying yes. Cassiane decided not to press the issue. She had to admit she was enjoying it more than she expected. She wished she'd planned it a little better, wished she had one of those harnesses she'd heard about but never had a chance to actually use.

"Be rougher," Con muttered. "Please."

Cassiane moved her hand from Con's hip to her ass. After a moment's hesitation, she lifted her hand up and brought it down with a loud slap. Con cried out, the word "yes!" just barely audible above the yelp. A shudder ran through her and she arched her back, moaning loudly and now moving hard against Cassiane.

"Don't stop," Con said again, her voice low and guttural. "God, please. Don't stop."

Cassiane spanked her again and Con hissed. Her whole body tensed as she came, and she released the edge of the desk and rolled her head back. Cassiane slid her hand free, the fingers now wet, and held Con's hips with both hands. She was still pressing tight against her so she could feel every twitch and tremor that shook the other woman's body in the aftermath.

"I think I just taught you something different than I intended."

Con laughed breathlessly and cleared her throat. "Thank you. Yes." She pushed herself up again and twisted to look at Cassiane. "It was, um. It..."

Cassiane saved her from finding the end of the sentence by

kissing her. She knew Con had her eyes open, but Cassiane kept hers closed. She stepped back and gave Con some distance to pull her pants back up.

"So," Cassiane said, clearing her throat, "my point was moments like that are rare, precious, and necessary. It helps us keep our humanity while we're doing awful things."

"Lesson learned. And I've also learned that maybe we have different opinions about what men can offer. Thank you for that as well." Con touched her neck, then smoothed her hand over her hair. "Um. If that happens again, you..." Her voice trailed off.

Cassiane said, "Go on."

"Pull my hair." She coughed and looked away, her hand on her chin as if the words had fallen out and she had to wipe them away.

Cassiane smiled. "I'll keep it in mind."

Con excused herself to use the restroom. Cassiane pulled the chair back to the desk and sat down. She rearranged the papers Con had scattered during their impromptu fucking, trying to see if she could make any sense of the cypher. It was a vast understatement to say codes weren't her area of expertise, but Con and Timo had both hacked away at it enough there was a chance she might see a pattern where they didn't.

Con came back with her hair wet and slicked back out of her face. She nodded at the cypher. "Making any progress?"

"No," Cassiane said, "but it takes me the whole day to do the Sunday Jumble, too."

Con laughed softly and went to the couch to lie down. "I've never been treated like that before," she said once she had settled on the cushions. She directed the statement at the ceiling. Cassiane remained silent. "I've never been treated like I was last night, either. Or the time with Timo. They were all such different experiences, but all of them were... they..."

"Are you objecting?"

"Not in the slightest. I want to do it all again. I want to be with you the way I was with Timo. I want Timo to do the things you did." She squirmed and smiled, then put her arm across her forehead. "I want everything. All of it. Both of you. I never thought that would be an option and now I feel like anything else would be a disappointment."

Cassiane started to reply but was interrupted by the phone on her receptionist's desk ringing. She stood and crossed the room in four strides, gently pushing Con out of her way as she took a seat.

She pressed her lips together and squeezed her eyes closed as she lifted the receiver. When she spoke, her voice was airier and more relaxed. "This is Dr. Lippert's office, Sophia speaking." She could see the shock on Con's face but ignored it. "How may I help you?"

Timo said, "It's me." Cassiane turned on speakerphone so Con could hear as well. "I'm outside a coffee shop on Skalitzer. It's called Horvath and Keller. I'm surveilling someone I believe is waiting to meet Rudin. I followed him from a stronghold in the forest which I found at the coordinates from the letter."

Con went back into the office.

Cassiane watched her go. "What do you need from us?"

"First-aid kit would be nice. Not vital but I would like fresh bandages. Otherwise I don't want to risk spooking the guy. Right now he's just sitting at a table reading the newspaper. He looks up when people come inside but he doesn't seem overly impatient."

Con returned with the letter. "Timo, does the man have purple gloves on his table?"

"Yes," Timo said without hesitation.

Con put the letter down and pointed at one word. "I translated this into the Russian word for purple. Purpurnyy. Purple gloves didn't make any sense to me, but I was hoping there would be more context elsewhere in the passage. I think it's a signal. I don't think he knows what Rudin looks like."

Cassiane pursed her lips and considered that information.

"Circe, don't be stupid," Timo said. "Just bring the first-aid kit. He'll figure out that Rudin isn't coming and go back to the compound."

"And who knows where he'll go from there," Cassiane said. "Stay where you are, Timo. I'll be there soon."

"Circe!"

Cassiane disconnected the call and stood up quickly. To Con, she said, "Is there anything in that about what Rudin's signal is supposed to be?"

"I haven't found anything," Con said, "but I haven't translated the entire thing."

Rudin's suitcase was next to Timo's desk. Cassiane stood next to it and began undressing. Con watched her, a dubious expression on her face.

"What are you doing?"

"Getting ready. Go get the first-aid kit. It's downstairs. Bring it up here." Con remained where she was, so Cassiane snapped her fingers. "Now! Go! We don't know how long Rudin's contact will wait for him."

Con hurried to the filing cabinet and descended. Cassiane finished undressing and crouched next to Rudin's suitcase. It would be foolish to claim she *was* Rudin, but she couldn't present herself as she was. She needed a new persona. She didn't have time to create a character, not even enough time for a quick sketch of one, so she was going to dress entirely in his clothes: socks, underwear, cologne.

"My name is Josef Cisarov." She spoke again as she put on Rudin's underclothes, this time saying the words in Russian. And again as she stepped into his slacks, buttoned his shirt. She squared her shoulders and spoke the words in German with a Russian accent.

Con returned with the first-aid kit, which she placed on the desk along with a handful of other things: a watch, two rings, and a bracelet.

"I thought you might want... Jesus." She had apparently just noticed the transformation which had taken place in her absence. "You're pulling my trick."

"It was a good idea. What is this?" Cassiane picked up the watch, which she recognized as Rudin's. Her voice was deep, masculine, and spiced with just a hint of Russian inflection on the vowels. "Accessories. To help become him or someone like him. Yes. Very clever, Con. Thank you. Well done." She leaned in and impulsively kissed the younger woman's lips. Con flinched. "Everything okay?"

"Odd," Con said. "Just odd."

"Hopefully you won't have to get used to it. I don't expect Josef to stick around very long."

"Who..."

Cassiane thumped her chest. "Me. Josef."

"Oh." Con blushed. "After what we just did... seeing you as a man. It's..." She bit her bottom lip and her eyes shone. "It's good."

Cassiane smirked in a way she hoped was masculine. She put on a flat cap she'd found in the suitcase and gathered the items off the desk. Some of them she placed in her pockets, but the watch she strapped on. "Keep watch on him. If this truly is the meeting he's been waiting for, he may become desperate."

"You be careful as well."

Cassiane nodded and headed out to rendezvous with Timo.

CHAPTER TWENTY

TIMO HAD parked where she could see Barney through the shop's window, staying in the car so she could tend to her wounds. The cut on her shoulder was almost impossible to reach so she pressed it hard against the seat for as long as she felt was necessary for the bleeding to stop. Her arm was easier to treat, and had also bled more than she expected. Her right arm was smeared with red, and the entire heel of her hand was caked with it. She cleaned it off the best she could and wrapped her arm with a strip of cloth from her jacket's lining.

She had called Cassiane and Con from a payphone on the corner. When she got back to Horvath and Keller, she went inside to buy a something to drink and get a closer look at Barney. She had seen the purple gloves when he got out of his car but she wanted to see the man himself. She paid for her coffee and scanned the other patrons as casually as possible, never letting her gaze linger on anyone in particularly. She swept past Barney once, then again, and finally back for one last look.

He was older than she originally thought, his eyes and mouth lined with small wrinkles. He was good at acting casual, being just another stranger in a coffee shop. But she saw the way he examined everyone who came in, the extra second spent lingering when it was a man. She could see his posture straighten slightly as he waited for someone to react to the gloves on the table.

Timo took her coffee to a seat near the window. Twenty

minutes after she sat down, Barney had become visibly agitated. He had closed his newspaper and checked his watch multiple times per minute. He seemed angry at everyone who entered and ignored his purple gloves. She guessed he was moments away from leaving when the door chime rang again and a man in a suit entered the shop.

His clothes were too big for him, but they weren't baggy. His shoulders were wide enough for the jacket even if the sleeves seemed just a bit too long. He wore a hat with the brim pulled low over his eyes. He scanned the room and locked eyes on Barney's table. It was only then that Timo looked at the face closely enough to recognize it was Cassiane. She felt a jolt of surprise, twisted inside a surge of arousal. Cassiane was extremely handsome, and Timo was stunned that she'd made such a transformation in the short time since the phone call. She even moved like a man, all shoulders and long strides.

Cassiane approached the table and pulled out a chair without hesitation. Barney stared hard at her, unblinking, lips tight. She crossed her arms over her chest and looked pointedly at the gloves. Timo focused on them so she could hear what they were saying over the low murmur of conversation elsewhere in the shop.

"Rudin?" Barney said.

"No," Cassiane said. "My name is Josef Cisarov. I am an associate of Mr. Rudin."

Barney moved to stand up, but Cassiane leaned forward.

"Sit down. Our friend has been sitting alone in his hotel room for days now, with only a weeks-old letter to reassure him that this meeting would even happen. He has no idea what might have changed in that time. We can't even guarantee you're the man who sent the letter. If this is a trap, I told Pavel it would be better if I was the one who walked into it. Reassure me you are who you claim to be and we'll continue this properly."

For a moment, Barney remained poised to leave. Finally he lowered himself back into his seat. He scanned the room and the focused on Cassiane.

"You have brought the item which we discussed?"

"It's in Berlin," Cassiane said, still keeping her cards close to her chest. "I assume you are prepared as well?"

Barney dipped his chin affirmatively. "We're ready to proceed as soon as you provide..."

Cassiane put one finger on the table and drew the letter A. Barney nodded again. Timo watched his demeanor change. His irritation was replaced with an eager excitement. He leaned forward, eyes darting, voice lowering even further so she could only make out a few words.

"...take me to... deliver... begin immediately."

Cassiane remained impassive. "I want more than your reassurances. Rudin took a great risk bringing you the item. He is not going to hand it over to someone just because he has the right gloves. I need to see it with my own eyes, I need to tell him without a doubt you are the person who wrote the letter. The person in whom he put his faith."

"Faith means belief in the absence of proof," Barney said.

Cassiane smiled condescendingly at him. "I think we're well beyond that now. Faith has gotten us this far. It's time for something more."

They stared at each other across the table for a long, tense moment. Finally, Cassiane held up her hands in surrender and stood up.

"Very well. As long as there is doubt, Mr. Rudin would prefer to have wasted his time than risk handing over something so dangerous to the wrong person. Good day."

She turned her back and walked to the door. Barney stood up and pursued him. "Wait," he hissed. He clapped a hand on Cassiane's shoulder and turned her around. "Just wait." He looked at the patrons nearby, none of whom seemed to be paying any attention to the scenario playing out next to their tables. Barney lowered his voice. "I will take you there so you can see for yourself. You can report to our mutual friend that everything is as we promised in our correspondence. We have come too far to let distrust stop us now."

Cassiane didn't respond immediately. She hesitated, she looked out the window as a car passed, and finally looked at Barney again.

"What should I call you? Your true name."

Barney smiled. "The name is Salerno, friend. Grover Salerno. Come, we will go immediately. Rudin has waited long enough, and there is no reason to delay further."

He put an arm around Cassiane's shoulders to guide her out of the coffee shop.

Timo waited until they would be in their car before she followed them out. She didn't have to rush because she knew where they were going, and she could catch up without being spotted. She also had time to swing by the office and pick up Con. She didn't know what would happen when Cassiane and Salerno arrived at the compound, but she wanted to have all hands on deck just in case. It would mean leaving Rudin unguarded, but that was a risk they would just have to take.

When she got to her car, she saw that Cassiane had left the first-aid kit on top of the driver's side tire. She smiled and retrieved it before she got behind the wheel. She would let Con drive to the compound so she could re-dress her wounds on the way.

Salerno escorted Cassiane to his car, still leading the way even though he tried twice to lag behind and let her get ahead of him. She wasn't going to turn her back on him if she could help it. After the second failed attempt, he realized she knew what he was doing and gave up. She assumed Timo was following them but didn't risk ever looking in her direction in the coffee shop. Salerno was already suspicious enough without giving him conspiracies to grab hold of.

"I hope this isn't a long trip," she said as she got into the car. "Pavel is eager to be finished with this entire experience. He never adequately explained to me why you were delaying so long."

"Things had to be put into place." Salerno pulled away from the curb. "Rudin never mentioned an associate in any of his letters."

Cassiane said, "And I'm certain you didn't tell him everything about your side of the operation. Surely you don't think he managed this endeavor all by himself. The toxin he's offering is not the product of a single man's work. There are several of us who believe in this cause, Mr. Salerno."

He flexed his fingers on the steering wheel. "There are those who would call us agents of terror."

"The same people who inflict terror on us." Cassiane made sure to give the words an extra sneer of distaste. "Wars are not fought between heroes and villains. They're fought between two sides who are convinced their enemy is evil and must be stopped. We are not on the 'bad' side, we are on *our* side."

Salerno nodded thoughtfully. "We will be there soon."

"Good."

Cassiane looked out the window and watched the city fall away, quickly replaced by wilderness. She was unsurprised by Salerno's suspicion. It would be odd if he had taken her at face value. But now that they were alone, heading out of civilization to God-knew-where, she couldn't help but fear she had walked into a trap. There might have been a code phrase or signal in Rudin's letters that she'd failed to give. Salerno might know she was an enemy agent and was simply taking her somewhere he could eliminate her without witnesses.

It hardly mattered now. The die was cast, and she was on her way to whatever was at the end of the road. She would have to be prepared for any possibility once they arrived.

Timo came into the office at a full run, ignoring Con who shot up from behind the desk as if she had been caught doing something illicit. Timo went to the medicine cabinet and flung the door open, scanning the contents. "Go downstairs and collect the weapons," Timo said to Con. She chose a bottle and examined the label.

"What's going on? What do you need?"

"Cassiane is with one of the men Rudin planned to meet. I know where they're going, so I don't have to tail them, but the longer it takes me here, the more time she doesn't have backup. You're coming with me. So I need something that will knock out Rudin for the duration he'll be here alone."

Con said, "You actually know what all of these drugs do?"

"Of course not," Timo said. "But almost all antipsychotics have drowsiness as a side effect. I just have to find one that won't also give him diarrhea. I refuse to clean that up." She chose a bottle and put her hand on Con's shoulder to urge her toward the cabinet. "Go, go. Weapons. Extra ammunition. I believe there are only two men at the fortress, but we can't count on that. Hurry."

They climbed down into the basement. Con went to the weapon closet while Timo prepped the syringe. She held it low by her side as she unlocked the door to the ghost station and stepped inside.

Rudin grimaced and twisted his head away when she turned on the light, his entire body tense. She had no doubt he was stiff from being tied down to the chair for so long, but they couldn't exactly allow him time to exercise.

"I was beginning to worry you had forgotten about me."

"We could never forget about you, Pavel. Have you given any more thought to our offer?"

Rudin said, "Cigarettes."

Timo was surprised. "You've chosen?"

"No. Cigarettes. I suspected, but now I know that is how you drugged me. I do not know how, but that must be it. Very crafty.

Clever." He turned toward her, but didn't look at her face. His lips curled into a smile, which didn't make sense as a response to the syringe, but then Timo realized she had made two mistakes.

The first was that she hadn't changed her shirt before going downstairs. The sleeve was still wet with her blood. It was proof of a weakness which could be exploited.

The other was that they'd left Rudin alone too long.

He pulled both arms back, slipping them out of the restraints as easily as someone stepping out of a sandal. At some point he must have gotten free and then retied them looser so he could escape if an opportunity presented itself. Timo brought the syringe up but he slapped it away, then closed his hand around her injured arm. His fingernails dug into the cut and she cried out as pain shot up to her shoulder. Rudin crowded her and thrust his other hand forward against her chest. The blow was hard enough to make her miss a breath, and her heart stuttered at a peculiar rhythm for a moment. He forced her to her knees and closed his hand around her throat.

"If we don't do it to them, they will do it to us," Rudin growled. Through the fog in her vision, Timo could see tears in his eyes. "We will be destroyed, wiped off the face of the Earth, forgotten. We have to show them we will fight for survi--"

His looming presence was suddenly gone. Timo gasped and grabbed her throat as she watched Con haul Rudin toward the chair by twin handfuls of hair, using his weight as a ballast to swing them both around before she let go. His legs had gone out from underneath him so he tumbled like a paper bag in the wind. Con, meanwhile, moved like a dancer, landing on one foot and pouncing on him as soon as he came to a stop on the floor. He was face-up, and Con put her knee in the center of his chest. He grabbed the front of her shirt. She grabbed the sides of his head. She pulled him toward her like a lover desperate for a kiss, then shoved him back down. The back of his head rebounded off the tile floor, and one of them cracked loudly enough to echo.

"Jesus!" Timo croaked, scrambling to her feet.

Con slammed his head down again. His arms fell limp to either side, and now the tile under his head was painted with thick blood. She was muttering under her breath as she continued slamming him against the floor. Both his skull and the tile were cracked now, and there was no doubt that he was dead. Timo knelt beside Con and finally made out what she was saying.

"Motherfuckermotherfucker."

"Constance..."

Con twisted at the waist and threw a sloppy punch, her knuckles grazing across Timo's chin. Timo barely acknowledged the blow and wrapped Con in her arms. It was like hugging a tree but, after a moment, the tension went out of the blonde's body and she surrendered to the embrace. She exhaled sharply, a sob, and put her arms around Timo, clinging to her. Timo remembered the haze of killing people, doing what needed to be done in the name of the mission. She also remembered what happened when that haze lifted.

"What did I do?" Con whispered.

"You saved my life," Timo said.

They held each other for a moment longer before Timo leaned back. She moved her hands to Con's shoulders and looked into her eyes. There were specks of blood on her cheeks and forehead, some of it staining her eyebrow.

"Now let's go save Cassiane."

Con pressed her lips together and nodded.

They stood up together and Timo guided Con to the door. She looked back before leaving, partially to confirm Rudin was unmistakably dead and to confirm what she'd just witnessed had actually happened. Rudin's death was unfortunate but also necessary. She knew it would have come to this eventually. He wasn't likely to tell them anything useful, and they couldn't just let him go when the mission was over.

She could only hope he hadn't taken any vital information with him to the grave.

CHAPTER TWENTY-ONE

IT WOULD be generous to call the overgrown trail they turned down a "road." Cassiane was jostled and thrown in her seat as the tires rolled over clumps of shrubbery and roots that rose out of the ground like the backs of sea serpents. Salerno had barely said a word since leaving the city and her throat was grateful for the reprieve from speaking like a man. She kept an eye on the side mirror even though she didn't expect to see Timo behind them. Anyone in her position would have a fair amount of paranoia, and Salerno would find it odd if she didn't watch for a tail.

Finally they arrived at their destination. The wall appeared out of the woods ahead of them like a fairy-tale castle, the canopy overhead throwing a dappled shadow against the stone. Salerno slowed to a stop in front of the large wooden doors and beeped the horn once. They waited less than a minute before a dark-haired man pushed the door open. He paused when he realized Cassiane was also in the car, then resumed with a shake of his head. He stepped out of the way and Salerno rolled inside.

Cassiane examined the layout as casually as she could. Nothing much of note except for the helicopter. It was a Hind, a Mil Mi-24 attack gunship. The statistics rolled through her mind without effort: it could hold two main flight crew plus one technician, armor protection, accommodation for seven or eight fully armed troops, equipped with a gun, rockets, and guided missiles. Seeing it parked so casually near Berlin made her blood run cold. It explained why they had made Rudin wait so long. Getting it into position was probably an arduous task, even more difficult than one scientist getting to East Berlin with a chemical weapon.

Salerno parked and they both got out. Cassiane knew the other man had been following the car, but now she saw that he had drawn a gun. He was holding it by his hip but she didn't doubt he was prepared to use it.

"What the hell is this?" he asked Salerno in Russian.

"Relax," Salerno said in the same tongue. "This is Rudin's associate. He simply wants to put our mutual friend's mind at ease."

Cassiane switched to Russian as well. "I am unoffended by the weapon. I appreciate the attention to security."

The dark-haired man clenched his jaw.

Salerno chuckled. "Patrick Weldon, this is Josef Cisarov. Josef, Patrick."

Cassiane gestured at the barracks. "Are there more men in there, or is this the entire battalion?"

"We have all we need," Weldon said, answering without actually answering her question. He pointed at the helicopter. "And you've seen what you need to see. Proof that we fulfilled our part of the bargain. Now it is time for you and Rudin to prove you have followed through as well."

She turned and looked at the helicopter as if noticing it for the first time. She kept her expression neutral as she examined the barrels underneath each wing, but inside her mind raged. The armaments weren't guns, they were aerosol dispersal units. She tried to keep her breathing steady and walked closer, hands on her hips. The Hind had a range of only four hundred and fifty kilometers. But if they hopped from this spot to, say, Dortmund, then to Brussels, they could then go to France or England with no problem. Rudin's anthrax toxin, in these barrels, flown over a heavily populated area in Paris... her palms were sweaty as she imagined the cloud of poison drifting through London's streets.

"As promised." She was surprised her voice didn't shake.

"I would have expected more emotion," Weldon said.

Cassiane laughed and turned to face him. "Emotion?" She held out her hand. "My palms are sweating! We have been waiting for this moment for so very long. It's hard to believe it is finally here."

Salerno grinned. "As soon as we have your toxin, we will begin preparing for departure. We could be at our destination within twelve hours." He looked her in the eye. "We just need one final piece of the puzzle."

"Of course. We'll go get it right now if Mr. Salerno doesn't object to getting back on the road this quickly. But I think we're all impatient to complete this exchange."

Weldon finally brought the gun up. "I think Mr. Salerno does object to getting back on the road, actually."

"Patrick..." Salerno said.

"There's no need to waste time driving all the way back to the city just to pick up the package. There's a phone in the barracks. Call our friend Pavel, have him bring the toxin to us."

Cassiane smiled incredulously to hide her nerves. "Rudin has no vehicle. Even if he did, you truly expect me to tell him how to find this place over the phone? I haven't the slightest idea where we are!"

"After everything he has done for this mission, surely he will not draw the line at stealing a car. Grover can give him directions to find us." He leveled the gun at her head. "Go into the barracks right now and call him."

Cassiane looked at Salerno, who seemed reluctant but agreeable to his partner's plan. He shrugged and said, "The longer you hesitate, the more suspicious we become. It does seem like the most reasonable course of action."

"Fine." Cassiane started toward the barracks. "In the time it takes for you to explain where this place is, and for Pavel to find and steal a car, and accounting for how many times he will get lost in these woods before he finds this place, we could run into the city and pick him up. This is actually a *waste* of time. But if it will put your minds at ease..."

She had just stepped through the door when she heard running footsteps behind her. She turned so that Weldon slammed into her side rather than tackling her full-on, but the force still knocked her off her feet. She hit the floor with him on top of her, pinning her down, as Salerno shouted at Weldon. He sounded as shocked as Cassiane felt. She acted on instinct and shoved away the hand holding his gun, then shoved her other hand into his gut.

They grappled briefly on the floor. Weldon thrust his knee between her legs but didn't get the desired cry of pain. She closed her hand around his throat and squeezed. Salerno appeared in the doorway above them, eyes wide in shock. After a moment of indecision, he grabbed the back of Weldon's shirt and lifted him up, shoving him against the wall and holding him there with a hand in the center of his chest. Cassiane got to her feet and eyed the men warily.

"What in the blazes was that?" she demanded to know.

"Never over the phone!" Weldon said, jabbing a finger at her. "Rudin's own mandate. He did not trust the phone, not for a discussion of this, not for what we are doing. Absolutely no telephone conversations about this mission. Any true associate of his would have *walked* back to Berlin before agreeing to make a call."

Salerno looked at her as if he hoped she had a reasonable explanation. They were standing between her and the door. In the brief look she'd gotten of the barracks when she entered, she knew it was a single room with no other exits besides two windows on each wall. She would never get to them before one of the men shot her in the back.

Weldon apparently got tired of waiting and pushed Salerno's hand away. "You are not Pavel Rudin's associate. So who the hell are you, and why should we let you keep breathing?"

Cassiane abandoned her male persona and held her hands up in surrender. "I'm the only person in Germany who knows where your anthrax is, and the only person who can get it to you."

They looked at each other. Salerno took out his gun and aimed it at her. Weldon brought his gun up as well. Cassiane, unphased, smiled at them.

"You can call me Circe."

Timo only spoke to give directions, and Con followed as silently as an automaton. She checked her wounds and redressed the bandage on her arm. When they arrived at the turnoff where she'd seen Barney's car emerge, she told Con to take it. There was no need to go traipsing through the wilderness this time, especially not when her agent was in danger. No... not her agent. She didn't know what Cassiane and Con were to her, but they were both more than that now. She cared about them both, and she was anxious about what could be happening in the fortress. She was just as anxious about what was going through Con's mind.

"You did what had to be done."

Con's shoulders tensed. "What?"

"Rudin," Timo said. "There was no getting out of that situation without one of us dying. Or him killing you and me, then escaping. I don't want you to feel guilty for doing what was necessary."

"Oh." She blinked. "I'm not. I've done it before."

"You have? You don't seem... I only mean, I assumed you normally stayed behind the scenes and let agents like Cassiane deal with that sort of thing."

Con nodded. "I do. Whenever possible. But sometimes it's unavoidable. Like you said. Things have to be done. But I'm... good at it. I like it." She looked at Timo but then quickly faced forward again before they could lock eyes. "It's the same thing that happened with the hotel manager. Ernst. I could have tried bribing him or convinced him to look the other way. But he was a person who wouldn't be missed, so I... put an end to him. I don't regret it and I won't lose sleep over it."

Timo said, "That... isn't necessarily a bad thing."

"No, it is. It is. That's like telling an alcoholic that one beer won't hurt. It's why I remove myself from the possibility of violence as much as possible. If we had a larger team, I could have stepped back to let someone else take care of it. We weren't that fortunate."

Timo put her hand on Con's thigh. "From my point of view, we were very fortunate to have you here. For several reasons."

Con looked at Timo again, this time meeting her gaze.

"We're almost there, I think," Timo said, looking away.

"What is the plan when we arrive?" Con said. "I doubt there is a doorbell installed in this fortress you described."

"Not that I saw, no." She could see the wall through the trees now. "The car isn't high enough to use as a ladder to get over the wall. Even if we could, the broken glass embedded in it would cause problems."

"You saw the inside of the door. How secure is it?"

"What do you mean?"

Con said, "The security measures. Is it a bar across the center of the door, locking it from side to side?"

Timo closed her eyes and pictured it. "No. There are two rods sticking down into the ground. They extend up, about two meters from the ground."

"Damn," Con said. "That would likely prevent us from ramming it."

Timo tilted her head to the side. "Why?"

Con shrugged as if the answer was obvious. "Ram it at top speed, those rods are most likely sturdy enough to remain planted. They would crush the front of the car and stop it from knocking down the door."

"That doesn't mean we can't ram it..."

"What?"

They were parked in front of the wall now. Timo chewed her bottom lip and twisted to look out the back window.

"Back up far enough to get a good speed. And unfasten your seatbelt. We're going to have to jump."

Con looked concerned, but she put the car in reverse.

"American?"

Cassiane only stared, once again refusing to answer, so Weldon punched her once again. Her lips were split, her nose bloody, and she assumed she would have a fine quilt of bruises all over her face if she survived long enough for them to bloom. Weldon, currently pacing in front of her with both sleeves rolled up, had been polite enough to attack both sides of her face equally so they would probably swell in a uniform way. She appreciated that. She liked symmetry.

"British?"

"You did that one already," she said, receiving another punch for her trouble. Her body swung with the force of the blow and she thumped against the wall before swinging back to where she started. Her arms were secured above her head, tied to a closet rod. She grunted and shook her head. "Hey, what do you call those things... the things on a clock, the ones that swing..."

"Pendulum?" Salerno said from the back of the room, where he was keeping his hands clean.

"That's it. Thank you." She looked at Weldon. "Anyway, continue. You haven't asked if I'm Spanish yet."

He punched her hard and she laughed as she swung again. "Yeah." It hurt her lips to talk, and she tasted blood. "Pendulum. That's it."

"I've had enough of this," Weldon muttered. He walked to a pack next to one of the beds and pulled out a medium-sized hunting knife with a wide blade, the end almost blunt on either side of the tip. He held it up to be sure she saw it as he approached. "I'm done trying to make you talk. I just want to hear you scream now."

"How big is that thing, four inches?" She clucked her tongue. "Someone is compensating for something."

He swung the knife and sliced her thigh, a move so sudden that it took a moment for her brain to realize she'd been injured.

The dull throb became sharp and hot, but she didn't react to it.

"Giving up already? There are so many other countries you didn't guess. Egypt. Greece. Brazil."

Weldon stabbed her in the side.

Cassiane went still, focused on a spot just over his shoulder. He hadn't stabbed her very deeply, but the wound was definitely not something she could just shrug off. Blood spilled down her stomach, pooled inside her shirt. She was aware of the situation's irony. Not twelve hours ago, she had been advocating for rough treatment of prisoners. And now... now...

"I guess that finally shut you up," Weldon said.

Salerno said, "This isn't helping."

"There's nothing she can do to help," Weldon said. "She's not giving us information about who she is. She won't tell us how she knew so much about what we're planning. She won't tell us why Rudin didn't come to the meeting. It would seem we have to abort the mission, and I am eager to get as much as I can out of it. Even if all I get is making this bitch suffer for getting in our way."

"Always happy to be of service." Cassiane was startled by how weak and shaky she sounded.

Weldon brought the knife up and cut her on each temple. It stung more than it hurt, but she could feel the blood trailing coldly down her cheeks.

"Maybe I could cut a line across your forehead. Blind you in blood."

Salerno said, "If we're going to kill her, let's just kill her. This is—"

"Sadistic," Weldon said. "The word is 'sadistic.' I don't like it, but I guess it's apt. I'm—"

He was interrupted by something crashing nearby. Salerno pulled out his gun and checked the window. "Something hit the gate."

"Is it still standing?"

"Yes."

Weldon said, "Go see what happened. Give your poor stomach a break from watching this terrible display."

Salerno grumbled but did as he was told.

Cassiane watched him go, then focused on Weldon. "I like the set-up you have here. I thought about something like this for Rudin. Let him dangle. All that stress on his joints, bound to make him more willing to talk."

"You talk too much." He cut her cheek.

"And you should have tied down my feet."

Cassiane swung her lower body up and wrapped her legs around his waist. He tried to pull away, but she locked her ankles behind him. He brought the knife down twice, slicing her hip and upper thigh. She refused to let go. She had formulated this plan as soon as they strung her up, but she couldn't risk it while Salerno was in the room and out of her reach.

Cassiane pulled him closer and slammed her head into his face, the slope of her forehead against the bridge of his nose. Blood gushed over his mouth and chin and he stumbled a bit. She did it again, which hurt her but dazed him enough that he dropped the knife. She released her legs and dropped her feet down. Her body swung back toward the wall. She put her foot against it and propelled herself forward. She brought her leg up and kicked him in the crotch.

Weldon threw himself at her. At the same time he impacted her, she pulled down with all her strength, and the clothes rod came free. They both collapsed on the floor and she rolled. He grabbed the knife. She wrapped her hand around his and twisted the wrist at an unnatural angle until she felt it pop. He howled. She took the knife. She twisted and buried the blade in his chest, pushing through the resistance of muscles until it sank to the hilt. His entire body convulsed and then went very still.

Cassiane was panting, all of her injuries screaming for attention as she squirmed away from him. She left pools and smears of her own blood in her wake.

"Not enough... people in your squad," she said, slumping down onto the floor to catch her breath. "It can be a problem... yeah... we had the same problem... It's... a problem."

Salerno didn't like any of this. He didn't like Patrick torturing this woman, even if she was an enemy agent. He didn't like that Rudin was missing without explanation and that they had no idea where the anthrax was. He'd never been terrifically happy with the mission in the first place, but he knew it was important. He was willing to do what was necessary to save his people, even if that meant getting his hands dirty. He knew he would be responsible for thousands of deaths, maybe more, but that was always theoretical. It was something completely different to watch a woman get cut and stabbed.

The main gate was intact, as he knew it would be. It was constructed to withstand impact from an armored truck. He prepared his gun and pushed the gate open just enough to see out. A sedan was wrecked just outside, its engine crumpled and belching thick clouds of smoke which obscured his view of the windshield. He scanned the area and cautiously approached the driver's side door. Someone was slumped against the steering wheel.

"Show me your hands!" he shouted in German. "Now!"

The bullet that killed him came from behind, so the only warning he was given was the flash of muzzle fire reflected in the car's windows.

Timo emerged from the woods as Con got out of the car. Barney's blood had splattered the driver's side door, but fortunately the window had been up and spared Con from being sprayed. She had gotten the car up to ramming speed and jumped out just before impact on the assumption that ejecting would be less dangerous than hitting a reinforced door at full speed. Judging from how she was standing, it seemed like it had been a lateral move.

"All right?" Timo asked.

"Sore," Con said. "But fine."

Timo led the way into the stronghold. Con retrieved a gun from the car and followed her, keeping an eye out for any other agents who might be lurking. Timo had only seen Fred and Barney, but the barracks looked big enough to house at least a half dozen men. She moved toward the barracks and motioned with her chin for Con to check out the other building. Con nodded, sweeping her weapon across the domed glass of the helicopter's cockpit as she passed it.

The barracks door was standing open. Timo pressed against the wall and, hearing silence from within, ducked around the corner. Two bodies were sprawled in the center of the space, both so bloody that at first she assumed they had both been beaten to death. One, Fred, had a wooden handle of a knife rising from the center of his chest. The other was facedown nearby, one arm stretched toward the door and the other tucked under her body. Cassiane.

Timo ran to her and put a hand on her shoulder. "Circe... can you hear me?"

Her body twitched. Cassiane tried to raise her head but failed, instead letting out a low moan. Timo moved her hand to put pressure on the worst of the wounds, but she couldn't even begin to prioritize any of the horrible injuries.

"Don't try to move, darling." She twisted at the waist and saw Con jogging toward them. "Anyone in the other building?"

Con shook her head. Her eyes widened when she got close enough to see Cassiane's body. "Radio and communications equipment. Good lord. Is she..."

"Alive," Timo said, then looked down at Cassiane and motioned for Con to join her. "For now, anyway. Let's see that she stays that way."

CHAPTER TWENTY-TWO

ONCE CASSIANE had been stabilized, Con brought Salerno's dead body into the compound. She also pushed their totaled sedan inside, even though it was highly doubtful it would be spotted. There was always the chance there were more agents stationed elsewhere who would eventually show up to check in. The damaged gate was already enough of a warning sign without leaving the car in plain sight.

Timo dug graves in the far corner for the men she'd called Fred and Barney. Con took stock of the garage, which served as kitchen and communication center. She found logs and records of conversations with their superiors. It was a treasure trove of information which could be used to track down the people behind the mission and prevent them from trying again.

Of course that wasn't their responsibility. She would report all of this to Command, who would assign a new team to follow through with the information. Their mission had been to eliminate the immediate threat posed by Rudin and his toxin, and they'd accomplished that. As soon as Cassiane was healthy enough to travel, they would leave.

Fortunately, most of Cassiane's injuries were superficial. The stab wound in her side was the worst of it, and they'd managed to stop the bleeding before it turned critical.

Three days after they'd raided the compound, they'd settled into an almost domestic routine. The soldiers had rations for at least three weeks, so they ate very well at every meal. Timo used Barney's car to go back into Berlin so she could send a message to Command - "Mission accomplished, await further instructions" - and returned with two bags full of their own clothes. Cassiane was confined to one of the beds while Con and Timo shared the other. On the third night, they made love while Cassiane watched. Con was surprised that the only part of it she found odd was the fact Cassiane wasn't joining them.

On the fifth day, Con was sitting on the front step of the barracks watching Timo examine the helicopter. The communication record was on her lap, but her eyes were too tired to keep reading. She was enjoying the sunshine and the fact Timo had stripped down to a sleeveless undershirt for her exploration. The sweat on her biceps was enough to send Con's mind off in a dozen different directions, all of them pleasant.

She heard shuffling footsteps behind her and scooted to one side to make room on the step. It took nearly two minutes for Cassiane to reach the door and take a seat, but she did it without help. Once she was settled, she exhaled hard and rubbed her bandaged thigh through her pants.

"Don't tell me I should be in bed."

"I didn't say anything," Con said.

Cassiane said, "I haven't been outside in almost a week. Meanwhile, the two of you..."

"We're not exactly out here picking daisies and playing with butterflies."

"But at least you're doing *something*."

Con reached over and rubbed Cassiane's leg, below the injury. "I know. It must be terrible for you to be laid up like this." She pressed her lips together and looked at Timo. "If I'm being totally honest, I'm not very sorry. I mean to say, yes, I'm sorry you were hurt. But the longer it takes for you to be mobile, the longer we can remain here together. When the mission is over, we'll get new assignments. New partners. This will end."

"Hm." Cassiane looked at the helicopter and they both watched Timo for a while. "You know, this is the second time Timothea has saved my life on this assignment. Twice I've been lying there practically dead and looked up to see her hovering over me. Have you ever had a near-death experience like that?"

Con shook her head. She wasn't used to hearing Cassiane talk this much and was loath to interrupt.

"I lost a lot of blood. I felt like I was floating. I couldn't focus on anything except when she was looking down at me, touching me. It hurt, you know? Having my wounds cleaned and sewn up. So every time she would touch me, it hurt, and it kept me from floating away. Even later when everything came back into focus, I still felt like I was levitating around her. Like I had one foot off the ground. I'm sure you know what I'm talking about."

"I do," Con said tentatively. "I don't intend to stand between the two of you~"

"Oh, stop," Cassiane said. "Has Timo suggested she wants us to fight over her?"

"No..."

"No. I see no point in choosing if no one wants to choose. I'm happy with things the way they are. When we get back, I don't see any reason to keep us apart. Maybe one of us will be sent to England for a mission, maybe two of us will end up in the same godforsaken post somewhere else, but when we're at home, when we're... ourselves... why can't we find each other? Be with each other?" She was looking at the ground now. "I know I would like that."

Con said, "I would, too. Very much." She moved her hand to Cassiane's shoulder, squeezed, and let it fall.

Timo looked over at them. She aimed a finger at Cassiane. "You should be in bed!"

Cassiane flipped her off.

Timo sighed and shook her head before she climbed back into the cockpit.

Con smiled, but it faded as her mind continued rolling. "Did... H-has Timo told you about what happened to Rudin?"

"Yes."

"What do you think?"

Cassiane didn't answer for a long time. "I don't think I think anything. I'm grateful you were there. What do you want me to think?"

"I hate that side of me. The violence. How much I en-enjoy it. I don't seek it out. I don't go out of my way to hurt people. But if it happens or if it's required..." She wrinkled her nose. "I like it when you hurt me while we're fucking, too."

Cassiane said, "Okay."

"That's all you have to say?" Con was nearly in tears. "It's a sickness."

"No," Cassiane said. "No, it's just who you are. The man who hurt me..." She tossed her head toward the barracks behind me. "He did it because it was fun. He liked hurting me. It wasn't even a cat toying with his food because even that has a purpose. This asshole, Patrick... what does Timo call him?"

"Fred."

"Right. Fred. He was doing it because he wanted to and because he could. That was a sickness. That isn't what you do and it's not who you are. You're a person who does what is necessary. It's an asset in this profession. Timo might be dead if it wasn't for you. And I certainly would be. Hurt the people who need to be hurt. Let people you trust hurt you when you're in the mood for it. Tell Timo to pull your hair. Tell her to choke you. She'll do it if you tell her it's something you want. And if you're both willing, then there's no reason to feel shame."

"Okay," Con said quietly. Then, a moment later and a little louder, she repeated it. "Okay. Thank you, Cassiane."

They sat silently and listened to the birds overhead.

"You know me."

"Hm?"

Cassiane cleared her throat and looked down at the ground between her boots. "This mission. I haven't had a cover for most of it. I mean, yes, Timo's receptionist, but I never really used that while you were here. You're one of the few people I've worked with who hasn't seen me with a mask or a fake identity. You've only known me."

Con said, "And somehow I still like you."

Cassiane laughed. It was a real, deep laugh, and Con was almost startled by it. Even Timo looked up from what she was doing and stared for a moment at the sound of it.

"Wonders never cease," Cassiane said.

"When we first met," Con said, "Timo said the covers you used were your armor. Maybe that means you don't need armor when you're with me. With us."

Cassiane narrowed her eyes. "Maybe I do need it. I just don't want it."

A few minutes later, Timo left the helicopter and walked toward them. "I'm going into town to check for a response from Command. If there's anything you wish for me to pick up while I'm gone, have a list ready by the time I've changed clothes."

"I'm coming with you."

"You most certainly are not."

Cassiane was struggling to get up. "I'm going insane sitting here on my ass. At least let me sit in the damn car instead of lying in a bed."

Timo looked at Con, desperation in her eyes. "Will you talk some sense into her?"

"I don't refuse many missions," Con said, "but that is one I will not attempt."

"Useless," Timo said, resigned. "Very well. Come with me. I'll help you get dressed so you don't look like you just stumbled out of a war zone."

Cassiane looked at Constance. "I don't look that bad."

Con shrugged and looked away from her. Cassiane grunted. Cassiane got to her feet and limped back into the barracks. Timo looked at Con again.

"Will you be okay here alone?"

"Mm-hmm."

Timo said, "Okay. We'll try to be quick."

She went inside and Con tilted her head back. The sky was an unbroken blue above the canopy of trees, like little shining gems caught in the branches.

"Levitating," she said under her breath, then chuckled softly. She crossed her arms over her knees and put her head down.

She could definitely get used to levitating.

EPILOGUE

Six years later

TIMOTHEA HAD been awake for fifteen or twenty minutes listening to the rain, one hand under the pillow to push it up against her face so the grey light through the window wouldn't disturb her. Constance always threw open the curtains when she got up. It was one of her many annoying habits that Timothea refused to comment on because it would make Constance sad, and she hated to be the one who made sweet Constance sad. Besides, it did usually help her get out of bed.

This morning, however, she was reluctant to ever leave the comfortable nest which had been built around her. Twin concavities in the mattress on either side of her, the thick blankets tossed over her from both sides of the bed so that she was buried underneath a pile of it. It was one reason she loved being in the middle. It was Friday and she planned to have a long, lazy weekend that started with a solid twelve hours in their bed.

Her right ear, the good ear, was pressed into the pillow, so the sound of someone coming into the room was even more muffled than usual. She heard the humming drone of Constance's voice against her ruined eardrum as the blankets were pushed up so her toes could be pinched and pulled. She lifted her head but didn't open her eyes.

"Today is a sleeping day."

"No, it is very much not." She reached higher and swatted

Timothea's rear end through the blankets. "Get up. Come downstairs. There's something you need to see on television."

"Fine, fine."

Constance released her and went to the door. "Hurry. I don't know how long they're going to stay on it."

"Stay on what?" Timothea muttered.

She scooted to the edge of the bed and slipped into her robe. At least the house smelled like coffee, which meant getting up would have at least one benefit beyond whatever had Constance so excited. She put on her glasses but didn't bother with her hearing aid. Her left ear had been rendered next to useless when a car exploded next to her in '85, but she was learning how to deal with the loss.

Downstairs, Cassiane was standing in front of the television, arms crossed over her chest, an inscrutable expression on her face. Her hair was cut short and tending toward gray around the ears. She was already in her overalls for work, the gloves tucked under her belt, but something had made her stop on her way out the door. Constance was perched on the edge of the couch with the remote control in her hand.

Timothea felt a twinge of worry as she came around and looked at the screen. She saw Tom Brokaw standing in front of a huge crowd, his monotone voice raised to be heard above the mob surging behind him like an ocean wave.

"What's going on?"

"Berlin," Cassiane said. "The Wall."

Timothea stared as the journalist's words pierced her still sleep-fogged brain. The Berlin Wall was coming down. People were pushing over the border from East Berlin into the West. She'd been half-expecting something like this to eventually happen, but she thought it was months away. How could something so historic happen overnight, in the blink of an eye? But now they were showing the Wall itself, and people were actually passing through the checkpoints.

"God," she said. "Is this real?"

Constance said, "It would seem to be."

"This is happening now?"

"Last night," Cassiane said.

They'd gone to bed without watching any television. The one night she hadn't insisted on watching the news. She remembered arriving in East Berlin, remembered sitting silently beside Cassiane when she was still just "Miss Jurick." The first time they'd made love, the first time they met Constance. That awful, ugly city was where her life changed forever and now it was on the verge of being reborn. She went to Cassiane and held out her hand. Cassiane took it and squeezed.

Those terrible dark days of the Rudin assignment felt like a thousand years ago. She and Constance still worked for the KYP, but only desk work. Timothea's partial deafness made her superiors reluctant to send her out into the field, and Constance requested reassignment to a job which wouldn't require her to tap into the darker side of her nature. They worked together at the National Intelligence Service headquarters in Athens in different departments. Everyone they worked with knew they were "friends," knew they lived together and ate lunch together in the courtyard every day. They also knew they shared the house with Cassiane, an agent who retired before her luck could run out.

Before leaving Berlin, Timothea had burned most of what they couldn't carry out of the city with them. Cassiane had shirts, trousers, underwear, and socks that were completely ruined because of the blood staining the material. She could have worn an entire outfit which was covered with her own blood.

"Can you hear that behind him?" Constance said. "The tap-tap? They're chipping away at the Wall with tools. Saws, pickaxes. Like woodpeckers."

"Imagine that," Timothea said softly.

Constance said, "I couldn't have imagined anything that's happened in the past few years. A Wall being torn down is hardly at the top of my list."

Timothea smiled and glanced at Cassiane. She wasn't smiling, but there was a look in her eye that only Timothea and Constance seemed able to decipher. It was like speaking a rare language, one that only they could translate, and it made what they had even more special.

"I should get to work." Cassiane brought Timothea's hand to her lips and kissed the back of it. "I'm already late."

"We'll pick up dinner on our way back from the office."

"Not from that chicken place."

Constance said, "I like that place."

"They dry out the chicken." Cassiane went to the couch. She bent down and kissed Constance's lips. "If you want something from there, just get me the vegetables. That will be fine."

"We'll compromise," Constance said. "We love you."

"I love you back," Cassiane said, pausing to kiss Timothea on her way out the door.

When she was gone, Timothea said, "I like the chicken place. We can get that for lunch."

"Excellent plan." She muted the television and stood. "You take a shower and get dressed. I'll make you coffee."

Timothea intended to go back upstairs and follow Constance's plan, but she was distracted by the windows next to the stairs. The rain had tapered off and the sun was trying to break through. She went into the front hall and looked outside at their quiet suburban street. In a way, they were still living their covert lives. To their neighbors, they were just three single friends who happened to share a house. If the truth was ever discovered, it would cost them their jobs and force them to find somewhere else to live. The lies seemed smaller but the stakes were so much higher.

"I don't hear the shower running!" Constance called from the kitchen.

Timothea smiled and pulled herself away from the window.

It seemed as if a new world was being born, and from where she stood, it was definitely a world worth fighting for.

About the Author

Geonn Cannon lives in Oklahoma. He is the author of several novels, including the Riley Parra series which is currently being produced as a webseries for Tello Films, and an official Stargate SG-1 tie-in novel. Information about his other novels and an archive of free stories can be found online at geonncannon.com.

9 781944 591540